"I DON'T WANT YOU CRACKING ANY MORE JOKES AT MY expense," Allison insisted. "I don't want you touching my things. And I don't want you—"

"Oh, yes you do. And I want you," Reilly said firmly. Without warning, he pulled her hips hard against him, then brought his face close to hers. "I want you, Allison. All that fire in your eyes isn't anger, it's passion. Hot and heavy, singing out to me. And every inch of me is hearing you." He brushed her lips once. "We want each other. Like cats want cream."

"Cream? Why, you arrogant—"

Before she could get another word out, he silenced her with a long and stolen kiss. He asked for the next with a whisper of her name. Allison sighed. That kiss and more were already his. . . .

WHAT ARE *LOVESWEPT* ROMANCES?

They are stories of true romance and touching emotion. We believe those two very important ingredients are constants in our highly sensual and very believable stories in the LOVESWEPT line. Our goal is to give you, the reader, stories of consistently high quality that may sometimes make you laugh, sometimes make you cry, but are always fresh and creative and contain many delightful surprises within their pages.

Most romance fans read an enormous number of books. Those they truly love, they keep. Others may be traded with friends and soon forgotten. We hope that each LOVESWEPT romance will be a treasure—a "keeper." We will always try to publish

LOVE STORIES YOU'LL NEVER FORGET BY AUTHORS YOU'LL ALWAYS REMEMBER

The Editors

Loveswept® 638

TROUBLE IN PARADISE

SUSAN CONNELL

BANTAM BOOKS
NEW YORK · TORONTO · LONDON · SYDNEY · AUCKLAND

TROUBLE IN PARADISE
A Bantam Book / September 1993

*If you would be interested in receiving protective vinyl covers for your
Loveswept books, please write to this address for information:*

> *Loveswept
> Bantam Books
> P.O. Box 985
> Hicksville, NY 11802*

ISBN 0-553-44338-0

Published simultaneously in the United States and Canada

PRINTED IN THE UNITED STATES OF AMERICA

OPM   0 9 8 7 6 5 4 3 2 1

For Edrie Henry, Roger Cohen,
and Mary Wolk.
*Blessed are the curious, for they
shall have adventures.*

TROUBLE IN
PARADISE

ONE

"I've heard of 'going native,' but isn't this pressing the point?"

The voice was distinctly disapproving, close to his hammock, and utterly female. Reilly Anderson lifted his hat enough to see an expensive pair of high-heeled shoes and a take-me-to-heaven set of legs beside him on the veranda. He had to be dreaming. Legs like these weren't seen in the rain forests of Central America. He knew. He'd looked.

"Have you lost your voice along with your mind?" she asked impatiently.

Reilly stirred. So he wasn't dreaming after all. "Who wants to know?"

He heard her gasp.

"Tony? Tony, is that you?"

The hem of her white linen skirt slid up her

thighs as she leaned down to peek under his hat. Twisting her head to get a better look at his face, she narrowed her gaze indignantly.

"You're not Tony," he heard her say over the roar of the float plane's engine. "I'm looking for Tony Church."

Reilly stared back at China-blue eyes and what could be the most gorgeous woman he'd seen in eight months. He wasn't sure, because she continued her accusing stare from a peculiar angle. Everything else seemed to confirm his suspicion, though. Tendrils of blond hair were slipping from her topknot and drooping like damp ribbons around her earrings, high cheekbones, and dewy complexion. Because she was bending at the waist, her necklace hung below her chin and away from her clingy silk blouse. Then there were those lips, shimmering like her stockinged legs but peach-colored, pouty, and . . . He closed his eyes, frowning at the physical reaction she'd triggered in him. She definitely belonged in his dreams, but she didn't belong at the Paradise Hotel.

Not if she was looking for Tony Church.

Throughout his perusal the float plane's roaring takeoff wiped out every sound. She'd been trying to ask him something and when he finally heard her, she was shouting. "Can you tell me where I can find him?"

Dropping his hat on the floor of the veranda, Reilly straddled the hammock and sat up. With less than a month to go, this was all he needed. An insistent outsider poking her pert little nose around for Tony. "What makes you think he's here?"

His deliberately quiet response startled her. Straightening up, she smoothed the long, thin strap of her shoulder bag. When she'd regained her composure and was about to speak, her gaze wandered to a place below his face. Her smile faded as her lips parted to take in a breath.

Reilly looked down to make certain his fly was zipped. No surprise there. Hell, except for nature calls, he hadn't had it unzipped for months. He looked up at her again and guessed his clothes were causing her gaping stare. The faded Hawaiian shirt with the ripped-out sleeves and no buttons had seen better days. "I said, what makes you think Tony Church is here?"

"I, uh . . ." she began. Blinking, she looked out toward the river. Her voice was suddenly businesslike. "The young boy I spoke to at the dock—you see? There he is now. When I asked about Tony, he pointed up here to the veranda. I thought you were Tony." She looked him squarely in the eye this time. "Obviously you couldn't be."

"Obviously," he agreed dryly, turning his head toward the water.

A barefoot, shorts-clad ten-year-old was doing his best to half drag, half carry three suitcases over the wooden walkway leading to the hotel. The boy staggered to the stairs with a smile plastered across his face. Reilly winked at him, then returned his attention to the woman. She had managed a smile, too, but it was sliding away as the boy dropped a piece of her luggage.

She reached out her hands in a vain attempt to caution him. "If you could be a little more careful with those, I'd appre—" She winced as each piece banged against the wide steps. "—ciate it." Under her breath she whispered to Reilly. "Can't you help him? He's so small."

Small, yes, but Reilly had seen him carry thirty-pound bundles balanced on his head. Still, her voice was tinged with concern. He checked out her legs again as he spoke. "Chico."

As his brown toes reached the veranda, Chico turned toward the hammock. "Yes, Reilly?"

"Don't carry so many at the same time."

"Okay, Reilly." The boy opened his arms and let the luggage drop. One of the suitcases hit the edge and popped open, scattering its contents while tumbling back down the steps.

"My clothes!" Hurrying by the boy, she headed down the steps, grabbing up her belongings as she went.

Reilly raised his eyebrows as the boy moved toward the hammock. "We've got to work on this bellhop thing, Chico."

Chico nodded earnestly. "Three suitcases, Reilly," he whispered, holding up three fingers. "She is good for business. We'll be good to this lady, Reilly. Then this one won't go away fast like the others. She will spend lots of money. No?"

Reilly eased his gaze from the seat of her white linen suit. He frowned, thinking about the complications her presence would bring to at least two areas of his life. His work and his libido.

"She won't be around long enough. And you won't, either, if you don't get a set of bed linens over to Room Two. *Rapido*."

As the boy scurried into the hotel, Reilly stood up, swung a leg over the hammock, and made his way across the veranda. The leggy blonde didn't look up. Flowery silk nightgowns, several swimsuits, and enough pastel panties and bras to fuel his dreams for a decade disappeared back into the suitcase. He sighed. She was moving way too fast, and he was enjoying the show way too much.

"I didn't catch the name," he said, heading down the steps. He surveyed the scene, then reached for something pink and lacy and intimate. Whatever the article was, the sheer material would surely dissolve in the afternoon rains.

"Please don't touch those," she said, snatching whatever it was from beneath his fingers. She continued gathering up the rest of her belongings. How many of those *things* had she packed? he wondered.

As if she'd heard the unvoiced question, she raised her head. Her glance landed on his bare chest, moved up to his face, and then veered sharply to the right. She was frowning again, and he knew why even before he looked at the hotel's sign behind him.

"Kind of takes your breath away, doesn't it?"

She shook her head. "I've never seen anything like it."

When he'd taken over the Paradise Hotel eight months ago, he'd had to pit his immediate goal against his years of marketing experience to leave the sign the way he'd found it. The results of the humid climate and parrot droppings had all but obliterated the red and gold letters, turning the thin wooden rectangle into something resembling a prop from a bad B-film. The realist in him had won out over his executive ego, and the sign had remained in its original deteriorating state.

"I'm trying my best to keep us out of the travel guides."

"I don't think you'll have much trouble there," she said dryly.

Shaking his head, Reilly pulled on his ponytail and snorted with amusement. The Paradise Hotel wasn't what he had in mind when he'd studied at the Wharton School, but he had to admit that he'd developed a soft spot for the place. Probably his brain, he concluded wryly. What the hell? If the dilapidated structure didn't have charm, it certainly had atmosphere. And the rain forest, still standing, leant it an exotic backdrop.

In an unguarded moment he turned to the woman beside him. From the roll of her eyes he knew she wouldn't be sticking around for long. Clearly she didn't share his feeling about the place. Good, he told himself while trying to absorb the small bump she'd delivered to the executive side of his ego. Yeah. Right. Fine with him. She looked like trouble anyway, and trouble was something he didn't need at this stage of the project.

He took a half-smoked cigar from his pocket and slid it between his teeth. If she disapproved of his shirt, he couldn't wait for her next reaction.

"Maybe I shouldn't hide this little jewel. I think I will get postcards made," he said, holding a match to the shredded end of the cigar. He drew in enough to turn the tip orange, and when she finally turned to him, he tried out his grin, the snaky one Chico assured him made children in the nearby village hiccup. Removing the cigar, he waved it toward the building. "Welcome to the Paradise Hotel. I'm Reilly Anderson." He rubbed his hairy chest, then extended his hand, palm up. "I didn't wear my tie."

"I noticed," she said with ladylike contempt. Taking a business card from her purse, she placed it in his hand. "I'm Allison Richards."

Without a glance he slipped the card into the torn shirt pocket and his cigar between his teeth.

And then the staring contest began.

It lasted too long. In that steady, China-blue stare he met his match. And he didn't like it. Especially since the mirrored determination came packaged in feathery framed eyes, a resolute tilt of a chin, and a mouth that he sensed was capable of constantly surprising him—if he let it. And then of course only in his dreams. Her look continued boring into him with enough feminine energy to blitz every masculine circuit in his six-foot-two-inch frame.

It was his turn to look away. What was happening to him? Heatstroke? He was feeling peculiarly disoriented. He almost expected to look down and see himself standing in a boardroom in his business suit and power tie instead of on a rotting wooden walkway in khaki shorts and half a shirt. Drawing on the cigar, he reminded himself that disapproval was what he'd spent the last eight months courting from anyone wandering into the Paradise Hotel. Why was he allowing *her* disapproval to get to him? For safety's sake he allowed himself to look at her shoes while he thought about it. But he couldn't keep his gaze from its upward journey. When he got past her hips and those perfectly shaped, just-big-enough breasts, he was no closer to an answer. In fact he wasn't sure of the question.

"Mr. Anderson, I have my reservations—"

He looked at her face. "We don't make reservations."

"I meant, I have misgivings about staying here. But since the plane left already, I'll have to spend the night."

"I think I can fit you in," he said as she scanned the ground for any stray possessions. He could understand wanting her in that instant, sexual way any man would want her. Even with the humidity at one hundred percent, her hair straying around her cheeks, and the sheen of perspiration lighting her brow, she still managed to look as if she'd been sculpted from a breath mint. He could even understand his uneasiness about her asking for Tony Church. One wrong word on that subject, and they could all end up in the river. What he couldn't understand was the frisson of alarm bounding merrily through his body. Pulling the cigar from his mouth, he muttered a sibilant curse. Eight relatively uneventful months had gone by, and with less than one to go, she walked in. There was trouble in paradise, and he had to get rid of it. Fast. Picking up a can of hair spray she'd missed, he *tsked* several times. "The mosquitoes love this stuff."

"Thank you." She snatched the can from his fingers, tossed it in with the rest of her belongings, and closed her suitcase. "We were talking about Tony Church, Mr. Anderson. It's very important that I find him."

Beyond the clearing a howler monkey let loose with a leaf-shaking growl. Allison Richards's purposeful expression softened as she scanned the jungle around them. Reilly didn't miss the growing excitement shimmering in her eyes. The first time most people heard a howler this near, they usually started from the sound. By the look on her face she was hoping for a chorus.

Perturbed at the pleasure her reaction was providing him, Reilly wrinkled his brow and tried sizing her up again. This time he vowed to do it more analytically.

She was on the thin side, but definitely fit-looking. Health-club-fit-looking, no doubt. Those silky pastel scraps she'd returned to her suitcase were bound to look like cellophane candy wrappers hugging her— Whoa! Pinching the bridge of his nose, he forced his thoughts to the other mind-blowing subject she'd presented him.

"What makes you think Tony Church is here?"

Looking back at him, she was all business again. "His letter. The return address was the

Paradise Hotel, in care of Selva Verde Airlines. I know he's been here."

"Well, he's gone."

"Mr. Anderson—"

"Reilly."

"Reilly." She offered him an economy smile, the one she probably reserved for the mail boy or her pedicurist. "Where did he go, and how do I get there?"

Allison clasped her hands behind her back and held on for dear life as Reilly Anderson's gaze roamed over her again. And again. Lord, she hoped he wouldn't stroke his chest anymore. Whether he realized it or not, each pass of his hand was an invitation for her to follow suit. Once she felt those tight curls spring back beneath *her* fingers, she'd want to test his biceps with a squeeze and run her knuckles over his smoothly shaved chin and cheeks. While her attention was focused on his face, she'd most certainly have to test those lips with her own. A quick, hard kiss to knock his socks off, if he'd been wearing any.

"Everything all right?" he asked.

"Perfectly all right," she assured him while her heart continued ricocheting off the insides of her rib cage. But everything wasn't all right. Something about Reilly Anderson's blunt attitude had shaken her composure. While she was trying to figure out how that had happened, a long-forgotten image began fighting its way to her consciousness. She couldn't quite make it out. Tucked away for years, the image continued calling out to her for recognition, demanding attention to a once-familiar scenario. More confused than ever, she struggled to understand the meaning behind the shred of memory and why it connected to this moment. And to Reilly Anderson. The image started gathering momentum, but Reilly's compelling presence challenged it every step of the way. The tug-of-war continued for several disturbing seconds. Pressing her fingers to her temple, she looked toward the jungle.

Reilly broke the spell. "It's the heat up here," he explained. "Follow me." Picking up her suitcase, he returned to the veranda and picked up two more.

Forcing the memory back, she hurried up after him. He was right. Of course it was the heat. No one was calling her. Reaching for the screen door, she jerked back when he kicked it open and went inside. As he tossed her suitcases into the corner of the lobby, she bit back a groan. She hadn't survived that river landing in a one-engine float plane only to have Reilly

Anderson stop her search. He knew something about Tony, and she wasn't going to blow her chances of finding out what by whining over scuffed luggage.

Following him through a pair of saloon-style doors, she walked into the Paradise Bar and Grill. At least that's what the unlit neon sign advertised. The place looked more like a storage area for used and abused bar furnishings. Even the overhead paddle fan dipped and swayed like a warped record album.

"Name your poison," he said, ducking under the bar and popping up on the other side.

"A lemonade, if you have it." He gave her a skeptical look as she slipped onto a barstool and crossed her legs. "Perhaps iced tea, then?"

"Perhaps not. Better make it bottled water or beer." After mashing his cigar in an empty peanut can, he pointed over his shoulder at a modest array of recognizable labels. "I don't offer my hard stuff until after sundown."

His hard stuff. After sundown. Inside and out she melted a little more. Swallowing with effort, she took her time wrapping the strap around her purse before placing it on the bar. Sure, all Reilly's body parts spelled stud with a capital *S*, but there had to be a better explanation for this overwhelming fascination. Squirming on the barstool, she reminded herself that she always stayed clear of such an irritating type of man. She settled instead for—no, that wasn't right—socialized with a more intellectual type of man. A responsible type. At the very least, a civilized man, who wore shoes and had buttons on his shirt and used them. And never, never wore his hair in a ponytail.

Trying to avoid looking at him, she thought long and hard about her present state. There had to be a deeper reason why desire was flooding through her like a rushing river. Fanning herself with her one hand, she decided to blame this mix of fascination and desire on the humidity. Didn't everyone blame things on the humidity when they didn't want to think about . . . deeper things? "Perrier would be fine."

"Yes, it certainly would," he said, pulling a nondescript bottle from the bar's refrigerator. "But all I can offer you is our house brand." He presented it for her inspection as if it were a bottle of fine wine. "Cholera free and cold."

Goad on, she wanted to tell him. *You're not going to win. As vice president of mortgage loans I've been goaded by the best. And I don't want to like you anyway!* Okay, so that attitude was childish, but Lord, how she wanted to shout it.

"See?" he said, tapping the bottle with one finger. "It has all those tiny bubbles too."

She saw. Like the proverbial jungle cat in those documentaries on the Discovery channel, he lazed around his lair in the midday heat, sleek and deceptively mellow. When the time came for action, she knew, he'd spring to it like an arrow from a bow. Direct and dangerous. Touching her fingers to her brow, she pulled in a long breath. The last thing she wanted to do was put herself into a situation she wasn't prepared to deal with. Not on any level. Reilly Anderson might be her only link to Tony. She couldn't risk losing that link over another smart-ass retort.

"Yes, I see," she said, keeping her voice neutral. The tension between them continued tightening. How was he doing that? How was he reaching inside her with nothing but those big green eyes and shaking the very core of her? She pressed her lips together, willing herself not to respond, but he had already hit his target. She looked at him again, letting the smile creep slowly up her face before she spoke.

"What more could a girl ask for?" Taking the glass container from him, her fingers brushed his. Her gaze drifted down to the big, strong hands that had cradled the bottle. Tiny scars and a few calluses couldn't hide their sensual potential. They waited, open and empty and more than capable of answering her last question.

"You tell me," he said, locking into her gaze.

"Just a clean glass, but I don't think I'd offend anyone if I drank straight from the bottle."

He leaned back against the low cabinet behind him and folded his arms. "Knock yourself out."

Unscrewing the cap, she lifted the bottle to her lips and drank. She hadn't realized how thirsty she was until she'd finished half the water. When she started to lower the bottle, she realized he'd been staring at her. The air in the room suddenly thickened, slowing her movements. She wiped her lips, and his green eyes crinkled at the corners.

"Go ahead," he said, daring her with a dip of his chin to take the bottle once more to her lips. "There's more where that came from."

She knew he was trying to unnerve her and that the only way to win this round was to accept his dare and finish the water. She also understood that by wrapping her lips around the bottle a second time, she'd be a willing party to an erotic charade. A charade he wanted her to perform for him again. She meant to slam the bottle on the bar, but in that same instant something arced between them. Something strong and vital and more stimulating than the touch of any of her lovers—few though they had been. She started to raise the bottle, but his eyes suddenly darkened. Pushing off the cabinet, he swiped it from her hand before it touched her lips.

"Slow down," he demanded, trying to hide the fact that he was breathing harder than he should have been.

She let what she knew was a shocked expression remain on her face. So he felt this desire, this fascination too. The knowledge invaded her body with a drugging heat, or maybe that came from his closeness. Just inches away. "Why?" she whispered. "It's so good."

He leaned toward her. Her eyelids fluttered shut. When she opened them a second later, he'd moved back, suddenly standing tall again. "Because I don't want you puking all over the bar."

That explanation brought her to her senses. It also appeared to bring Reilly Anderson to his. He kept his hips pressed to the bar as he picked her card out of his pocket. "So tell me,

Ms. Allison Richards, vice president of mortgage loans, why are you looking for Tony Church? Did he miss a house payment?"

"It's a personal matter."

"Yeah?"

"Do you know where he is?"

"Maybe I do and maybe I don't."

Without breaking their connected gaze, she pushed off the barstool and tucked her purse under her arm. "Forget I ever awakened you from your nap. I'm sure there's someone around here capable of answering my questions if you aren't."

The staccato sound of her heels filled his ears as she walked across the barroom and out the saloon doors. The sound tapped into a dormant part of him, stirring his competitive nature. Adrenaline surged through his veins as that neat linen suit covering her backside continued baiting him. For one strange instant the past eight months vanished, and he was back at Taylor Pharmaceuticals moving and shaking with the best of them. Could this be true? Did he miss his pinching collars? Coffee in a paper cup? A good scrap about profit margins? He would muse over those things later. Not now. He wasn't through with Allison. "You'll be wasting your breath, Mzzzzz Richards."

"No more than I'm wasting it with you," she shouted back. "And how do I get a room around here?"

He ducked under the bar and joined her in the lobby. "You sign that book and follow me," he said, picking up her suitcases. He watched her flip through the pages, lingering over a few near the end. When she began signing her name, he shifted the weight of the suitcases and turned to the door. "Don't bother filling in the rest of those blanks. I have your card. That's all I need."

She turned around and shrugged at the back of his head. "Why am I not surprised?"

"Beats me," he said, managing the veranda door with his toes.

She followed along, staring first at his hopelessly broad shoulders and the balling muscles of his arms and then at his behind, tight and compact—and begging for a pinch. Her eyes widened at the audacious thought. She'd never pinched a man's butt, but if she were so inclined, this was the butt to pinch. She couldn't help herself. She snorted a giggle and then another.

"Something funny back there?" he asked, turning the corner on the veranda.

"No."

He stopped at the second door and motioned with his chin for her to open it. Following her in, he dumped her suitcases on the floor. "Just a word of caution. People come to San Rafael for many reasons. Maybe Tony came to get away from something. Maybe he came to forget someone."

"Is that why you're here?" she asked.

If she only knew. He ignored the question. "Maybe Tony Church doesn't want to be found."

"Too bad, because, come hell or high water, I'm going to find him." She gave him her sweetest smile as she tossed her purse on the dresser.

"You're one determined woman," he said, shaking his head.

"I know Tony, and he'll want to hear what I have to tell him."

Reilly felt a trickle slide down his back. Damn heat. He reached to rub a low point on his spine. The trickling sensation continued even after he stopped rubbing. "Leave the message with me. I'll give it to him . . . if he passes through here again."

She shook her head. "I don't think so."

He shut the door with a backward push

from his foot. Moving a step closer, he lowered his voice. "I'll be discreet."

"I doubt that."

"Come on. What's this all about, Allison? What brought you all the way to San Rafael?" He leaned in close, but this time her eyelids didn't flutter shut. "What's the big secret? Is he in trouble with the law?"

She shook her head. "No, Reilly. He's going to be a daddy."

"What?!"

Reilly Anderson couldn't have looked more shocked if she'd sucker-punched him in the stomach. Or was it possible that his dazed expression was one of disappointment? Whatever was going on behind those deep-green eyes of his, she decided not to gloat. Reilly still hadn't told her what she needed to know. Perhaps this news would spur him to talk. "I said Tony Church is going to be a daddy."

His mouth opened and shut several times before he spoke. "How? I mean, when's the baby due?"

"In about four months."

"Four months?" he asked, staring at the neat gold belt buckle lying flat against her middle. "But you don't look pregnant."

"What?" Not me, you idiot. My sister. He's married to my sister."

His dumbfounded expression turned to relief and then to doubt. "Tony had never said anything about impending fatherhood."

"Of course not," she said, taking in the scene around her. Clean, folded sheets and a pillowcase lay on the unmade bed, a flashlight stood upright on the nightstand, and nothing large and leggy crawled in or out of anything. Convinced she could survive the night in this place, her gaze returned to Reilly. Her gaze always returned to Reilly.

"Allison, what do you mean by 'of course not'"?

"I mean, Susan didn't find out she was pregnant until after he'd left."

Raising his eyebrows, Reilly kept them up for several seconds before speaking. "How long after he left?"

"What kind of a question is that? Are you implying that my sister would lie about this?"

He ran his hand over his sleek hair and ponytail, then forced an apologetic grin across his face. "Sorry about that. Really." He cleared his throat. "So, how is Susan doing? Everything okay?"

This was an interesting turn. Reilly Anderson asking after her pregnant sister. She began answering without trying to hide her suspicion. "Everything's fine. A healthy textbook case, her obstetrician says." Adjusting her watch, she hesitated before telling him anymore. For once, instinct overrode her cautious nature, urging her to trust him. "Susan and Tony love each other very much. They just had a misunderstanding that somehow got out of control. Probably had a lot to do with all those hormones charging up in her." She wrinkled her nose. "You know how it is."

He wrinkled his. "No, I don't."

All those soft, sweet feelings welling up in her breast disappeared with his patronizing imitation of her. Off guard and confused, she mumbled, "Oh. Well, I don't either. I've just heard things." Damn him. Probably the only thing he knew about pregnancy was how to start one.

She watched him pull his hands down over his face and sigh with unnameable frustration. "Go home."

"Not on your life."

He gave her one long, unreadable look as rain suddenly banged onto the tin roof. "Drinks are at six, dinner . . . whenever," he said over the clattering noise above them.

Reaching for her wrist, he brought it close to his mouth. For a second she thought he was going to kiss the back of her hand. Instead he took a look at her watch, running his thumb along the delicate gold bangle, then capturing the mother-of-pearl face between his fingers. Allison, however, wasn't looking at her watch. The hand holding it and her wrist had captured her attention. The corded back of it was wide and tanned with a recent history written in fresh nicks and several scratches. Such a beautifully masculine hand; she'd never felt quite so fragile. With her heart booming loud enough to drown out the rain, those mysterious images were on the move again. As if it were an old tune fading in and out of her consciousness, she strained to hear the words, but no one was singing.

"That's in two hours," he was saying. Letting go of her wrist, he headed for the door. "You can share my bathroom. Just lock my door when you're in there and don't forget to unlock it when you're through."

"Just a minute. Did you say I could share your bathroom?"

With one hand on the door he turned around, bracing his fist on his hip. She sounded as if he'd invited her to commit murder with him. "Hey. I don't offer to share it with just anyone. If you don't think you can keep your things picked up in there, tell me now."

"Doesn't this room come with its own bath? I mean, I've never stayed in a hotel room without its own bath." Panicking now and not caring that he knew, she concluded, "I've never had to share a bathroom with a . . . strange man."

Reilly bit the inside of his cheek to keep from smiling. "Besides the public facility near the bar, there's only one other working bathroom. It's on the opposite side of the hotel. If you think I'm that strange, you can share with Reverend Phillips and the Bartolino sisters. And Mr. Garfield, when he's around."

"Who?" she asked, touching her temples. She gave him a tired shake of her head. "Never mind. I don't want to know. I'm sorry I asked."

Reilly watched her sink wearily onto her bed. Her travel and her troubles appeared to be catching up with her. She stared at her shoes, then leaned over to wipe dust from the tip of the taupe-colored leather. When she raised her head to look around the room, he fought his inclination to give her a gentle hug. She looked as if she needed one. Cripes, with one word of encouragement she'd probably wrap her arms around him and cry. And then regret it. "Take a nap. Meanwhile I'll see if I can find the mosquito netting for this room," he said, going out and shutting the door.

TWO

As he stuck paper umbrellas in the Bartolino sisters' drinks, he heard Allison coming along the veranda. He wasn't the only one who heard her. That purposeful stride, punctuated by her heels, was announcing her imminent arrival to everyone in the Paradise Bar and Grill. Six heads were already turned toward the doors when she pushed through them a few moments later. Half a step into the room, she froze. Staring straight at him, she appeared to be seeing him for the first time. Her expression changed to a nervous grin before returning to that determined look, making Reilly wonder what would happen next.

Ignoring the curious smiles she was receiving, Allison marched across the room and up to the bar where Reilly stood. Her see-through shirt billowed behind her light-blue, low-cut, body-hugging jumpsuit.

"What'll you have?" he asked Allison while handing two drinks to Chico and pointing him toward two middle-aged women.

"Those mushroomlike things removed from your shower. The little ruffly beige ones growing in the corner," she whispered. "And my own towel, if you don't mind. I had to use a corner of yours."

"Hmmm? Which corner?" he asked, pouring a good measure of gin into a glass. He looked up to see her cheeks turning a bright pink.

Her gaze quickly darted to the bottle in his hand. "I—I thought you said you didn't serve your hard stuff until after sundown."

"I fibbed a little."

Patting the back of her smooth French twist, she turned away from him only to find the rest of the people staring at her. "G-good evening," she stammered.

Ducking under the bar, Reilly came up next to her. He draped an arm around her shoulder, sweeping his other toward the rest of the people. "Allison Richards, meet your fellow guests. The Bartolino sisters from Nebraska. Pamela and Marilyn. Down here for a few weeks collecting butterflies. Reverend Phillips. He's writing an ecumenical cookbook and, in his spare time, saving souls in the village. He's also our cook. The last one left for a better-paying position. And Mr. Garfield. He returned this afternoon from one of his, uh, excursions."

As the group gave Allison a collective nod, Reilly gave her a jerking hug, a deliberate parody of the one he had almost given her in her room. Her hand flew up to his waist to steady herself against the sudden movement. Now he knew what her frantic touch felt like, a piece of heaven exploding on his skin.

He paused, pretending Allison needed the moment to recapture her composure. "Of course you remember Chico from this afternoon."

Chico folded his arms across his chest. "You didn't tip me, lady."

"I'll take care of that before I leave."

"Don't forget."

"I won't."

The Bartolino sisters giggled.

"Hello, everyone," Allison said in her best toastmistress voice. Moving out from under Reilly's arm, she distanced herself from his casual posturing. "I'm here looking for my brother-in-law, Tony Church. He probably stayed at the Paradise Hotel sometime during the last three months. Reilly thinks Tony might not want to be found, and he's not being very helpful. I'd appreciate any information any of you have on this matter."

"Family matter," Reilly said, drawing attention away from Allison. "And I suggest we all stay out of it."

"My sister's going to have their first child, and I think—"

"I think," interrupted Reilly, "that Tony Church will go home when he's ready."

Glaring at Reilly, Allison pulled a photograph from her pocket and handed it to one of the sisters. "Do any of you remember him?" she asked, wishing she had a better photo than this tiny one she'd cut from Tony's high school yearbook. Since Susan didn't know she was looking for Tony, Allison hadn't wanted to stir up suspicion by asking for a more recent one.

Marilyn spoke first. "Sorry, Allison. We haven't seen him. We just arrived two weeks ago."

"What about you, Reverend Phillips?" Pamela asked, passing the photograph to the white-haired man wearing the clerical collar,

Bermuda shorts, and glasses. "You've been here for several months."

Chico stood on his tiptoes to get a look, then shrugged dramatically.

The Reverend stared at the photo for a long time before answering. Allison held her breath when he raised his index finger. "Short fellow, red hair and beard?" he asked, beaming her a smile.

"No. Tall fellow, blond hair and mustache." Taking back the photo, she studied it closely. "Of course he could have a beard now."

Shaking his head, Reverend Phillips sniffed the air and muttered something about poached fish before disappearing into the kitchen with Chico. She walked over to where Mr. Garfield sat. "Would you take a look at this photo?"

"Awright, pretty momma." The man with the long sideburns and turned-up collar glanced at the photo, then stared at Allison. A nerve twitched in his upper lip. "Haven't seen him lately, but I haven't been around much lately."

The man remembered Tony. Allison glanced at Reilly long enough to register her small victory. Now she was getting somewhere, even if Reilly refused to acknowledge the fact.

How much polishing did that battered old bar need?

Mr. Garfield leaned in close. "I'm lookin' for someone myself."

"You're searching for someone too?"

"That's right, pretty momma. That's my job. That's what I'm here for." With a flick of his head a jelly-roll lock of hair settled lower on his forehead. "Once I've closed the file on my current case, maybe I could help you."

Allison's sudden optimism was turning to suspicion as she continued watching Reilly. Busily checking his supply of paper umbrellas, he refused to meet her stare. "Mr. Garfield," she said, not taking her eyes off Reilly, "what exactly is your current case?"

"I'm lookin' for the King, pretty momma."

Reilly gave nothing away except a quick lift of his eyebrows. That was enough. He was going to pay for this. Slowly. Horribly. And with a lot of yelling. She closed her eyes. "The King, as in Elvis, Mr. Garfield?"

"The one and only, pretty momma."

"No, thank you." She made the short walk back to the bar.

"He's harmless," Reilly whispered.

"I'm not."

"Oops."

"You know where my brother-in-law is, don't you?"

"I know he's not here," he said, opening a lime-green umbrella and dropping it into a glass with two plastic straws. "Gin and tonic. Your first one's on the house." Sliding it toward her, his voice dropped to an intimate level as he looked her in the eye. "Nurse it."

A double-dog dare, if she'd ever heard one. Picking up the drink, she slid her tongue under the straws, closing her lips around them with puckering precision. After a moment she lowered the glass, fluttered her lashes, and smiled. "Like that?"

"Just like that," he said, resting his chin in the cup of his hand. He sighed. "Want to try it again?"

"Want to tell me where Tony is?"

Frowning, Reilly stood up, reached for a towel, and began wiping down the bar.

"I mean it, Reilly," she said with barely controlled anger as she placed her palms flat on the bar. "I'm not leaving San Rafael until I've found Tony. My sister deserves a second chance with her husband." She leaned in closer. "Their baby deserves a father."

Her last remark hit too close to home. Balling the towel between his fists, he turned away to jam it on the ledge behind him. When he could force his jaw to unclench, he infused his voice with as much light-hearted charm as he could muster. "Come on, Al. Do you honestly think I'd clutter my mind with information on someone who came through here months ago?"

"Clutter your mind? What else is taking up so much space? Certainly not your dedication to the efficient running of this hotel. And that reminds me, the air-conditioning is off in my room."

"What air-conditioning?"

"Oh, brother," she said, picking up her drink and taking another sip. "I hate even to mention this, but you never gave me a key."

A bell tinkled in the background.

"Dinner's being served on the west veranda," Reilly announced to everyone. Pointing across the room to where the others were already heading, he fell in step behind Allison. "We don't bother with keys, Al. People keep losing them or forget to turn them in when they check out. Most of the guests are a modest lot with nothing much to steal anyway. You, on the other hand, stand out like one of Marilyn and Pamela's butterflies."

"I do not." Stopping dead in her tracks, she

stretched out her arms, looking at them and her body. "What did you mean by that?"

The screen door banged behind the sisters before Reilly moved closer and began his answer. "Your clothes," he said as she lowered her hands to her hips. "They look expensive." Easing forward, he made certain his thighs were pressing against her backside. "All of them."

Picturing her panties and bras strewn over the walkway earlier, Allison sucked in her cheeks and stared straight ahead. His body heat penetrated her legs and rear, causing a generous rush of blood to every erogenous place she possessed. Damn gin. Two sips and her eyelids were closing. Yes, it had to be the gin, because she'd already reasoned that Reilly wasn't her type.

Leaning down, Reilly breathed against her ear, then whispered words that warmed her in more ways than one. "What exactly did you have in mind when you were packing for this trip, Al?"

His touch was a light caress, but she started peeling his fingers away from her arms as if it were a bone-crunching grasp. Hurrying through the door, she pulled out a chair at the end of the long table. "Not that it's any of your business, but as soon as I locate Tony and inform him of his responsibilities, I have plans to fly on to Costa Rica. There's a lovely resort there with all sorts of amenities. And who said you could call me Al?"

"Loosen up," he said while seating the sisters. "We're all friends here. Right, ladies?"

"Right, Reilly," the sisters replied in unison, following it up with a double dose of laughter.

"Allison? Pamela and I were just saying how that shirt and the chopsticks in your hair make you resemble the *anartia amalthea linnaeus*," Marilyn said.

"You're the first one we've spotted," Pamela added before the giggling began again.

Allison thanked them for their compliment while Reilly, mugging innocently in her direction, took a chair at the opposite end of the table. She resisted the urge to mug back. There were, after all, certain behaviors adults did not engage in—even if they were dying to. Besides, she had other things to think about.

During dinner Allison reviewed the status of her search. Thus far the Paradise Hotel had been a resounding disappointment. She had hoped to find Tony there or at least find out where he'd gone. Staying on for a few days was never part of her plan, but Reilly Anderson knew more than he was telling. She glanced at him over a basket of bread, then quickly looked around the table to see if anyone had noticed. Under no circumstances would she stay around him a second longer than necessary. Like the dark jungle, she thought, his sensuality both attracted and frightened her. The compelling imagery only served to confuse her as her gaze drifted back to him.

"A little more pressure," Reilly was saying as he instructed Chico how to manage a knife and fork properly. "That's better. We'll have you eating down at the *palacio* with *el presidente* if you keep this up."

"I want to show *mi padre* first, Reilly," Chico said.

She found herself smiling at the scene until Reilly looked up and winked at her. Annoyance replaced the pleasure of watching him help the boy, and she returned her attention to her plate, stabbing into the mashed yucca with her fork.

Concentrating on revising her plans wasn't easy with the sisters discussing their butterfly collection in Latin and Reverend Phillips explaining, at leisure, how to bone river fish. All of that would have been crazy enough fare for anyone, but one soft smile from Reilly and images from her childhood started creeping in. Laying her fork aside, she watched the engaging pair at the other end of the table. Distant images swirled closer.

Her parents taking turns reading aloud from a storybook . . . sitting beside her at the movies . . . watching television . . . and she was holding her breath and her sister's hand . . . because the world was a wonderous place . . . shaking with laughter and love and . . . what?!

What was that sound?

Something rustled above her head. Reilly shushed the table. Everyone grew silent, focusing rapt attention on his towering figure. Allison shivered with anticipation as Reilly brought his finger to his pursed lips. She held her breath. Whatever was out there beyond the clearing, whatever terror might be near, she knew one thing. One extraordinary but primal truth. Reilly would save her. Looking over the platters of fish and vegetables and plantains, she gave herself up to the hypnotic wonder of her revelation.

Reilly waited until the time was right before he began the chirping sounds. Each time he stopped, the answering rustle above him increased. Smacking his lips several times, he called out softly, "Puddin' Head, Puddin' Head, come to daddy."

The capuchin monkey dropped out of the rush ceiling and onto Reilly's shoulder. Small, furred arms wrapped around his neck as the others at the table scolded Puddin' Head for his long absence. Apparently he had dropped in to dinner several times before.

Allison pressed her fingers to her mouth as a gasp broke from her throat. Tarzan. The images were all about Tarzan. Her beloved hero from childhood sat before her with a monkey on his shoulder, a boy at his side, and all that glorious jungle behind his perfectly gorgeous face and body. She could have sat there for hours staring longingly at him as every childhood fantasy came flooding back to her. How she'd treasured those stories, every word of them and every reaction she had for them. She hadn't thought about the books or movies or television shows in years.

"Cheetah?" she whispered, delighted beyond reason.

The little head lifted toward her, its tiny shining eyes blinking with curiosity.

"Puddin' Head," corrected Reilly, picking up a piece of fruit and rising from his chair.

The monkey hid behind Reilly's head, leaving a furry tail twitching against the muscles of his shoulder and two tiny paws pressed against his smoothly shaved jaw. As he reached Allison, Reilly continued making the strange, soothing sounds. He handed her a fig, then lowered himself beside the chair of his enchanted guest. Her eyes were widening in blissful expectation. She held the fig close to her chest.

"Don't let go of it," Reilly said. He began transferring the monkey onto her arm. The moment the monkey saw the fruit, he leaped onto the front of her clothes and grabbed for it. Allison froze, her fingers banding around the fig. The monkey's mad scramble ended with the fig pushed deeply into her cleavage and Puddin' Head frantically shoving his tiny paws in after it. With the monkey screaming in her face, Allison grabbed her chair and stopped breathing.

"It's okay," Reilly told her. "Just stay calm."

Making a lip-smacking sound, he caught the monkey's attention, then slipped two fingers into Allison's cleavage. Her eyes widened at the surprise invasion.

"Don't move," he said during his lip-smacking lullaby.

Stroking the firm, satiny cleft, he twisted his fingers, easing them closer to the fig. That would have been outrageous enough, but when he wiggled them between her breasts, she felt a corresponding vibration of pleasure quivering between her thighs. A tiny moan escaped her throat.

"Sorry, tight fit," Reilly murmured, keeping up the rhythmic pattern.

She groaned again as currents of terror and pleasure shot through her body.

"You're doing fine, Al." Smacking his lips at the monkey, he shoved his fingers deeper. "I think I've got it," he said as his fingers slipped over one stiffened nipple. His gaze left the monkey's and locked with hers. "Sorry." And then, "Here it comes."

The fruit popped out, the monkey reached and caught it, then ran screaming across the table. The rest of the group left the table to follow the monkey along the veranda.

With her elbows locked to her body and her hands clenching the chair, Allison dropped her head back in the only show of relief she could manage. Her breathless state continued as Reilly ran his fingers across the top of her breasts. With the terror removed, his gentle touch brought her close to the edge of rapture.

"Let's have a little look." He began easing down the top of her jumpsuit.

Let's have a little look? Was he crazy? Reilly had taken her to the edges of sanity, then dropped her back to earth with a thud. She came to her senses, slapping his hand away and standing up in one smooth movement.

"Don't you dare," she whispered fiercely, pushing past him.

"If you have a scratch, you should have it tended to immediately." He followed her to the group on the front veranda. When she pushed around them, he stopped. "Neglecting nicks and scratches in this climate can be dangerous."

"We know that. Go after her, Reilly," Chico said, pushing the man twice his size toward her. "She'll leave, and I won't get no money."

Reilly was on his way again, urged now by the rest of the group. The veranda wrapped around the hotel, and with Allison headed the long way to her room, he had time for one short detour. Grabbing mosquito netting and a first-aid kit from the storage room, he finally slowed his steps as he neared her door. Just another day at the Paradise Hotel, Reilly told himself, only this time one of his guests was going to murder him. He wasn't surprised, but he wondered how she was going to do it.

Before he had a chance to knock, she opened the door as if she'd been expecting him.

"Did Puddin' Head hurt you?" he asked, stepping inside and away from her dagger-shooting eyes. She slammed the door. He was in for it, not doubt about it.

"No, Puddin' Head did not hurt me."

"Good," he said, stepping barefoot onto her bed. After that monkey business at the table he planned to be in and out of her room as quickly as he could. Unfolding the mosquito netting, he was reaching to fasten it to the wire form above the bed when she whacked him on the hip.

"Puddin' Head scared the hell out of me!"

In a caressing voice he said, "Al, you're blowing this way out of proportion. You should relax. Let down your hair, or put it up in a ponytail like mine."

"Don't you dare lecture me after that dog-and-pony show. What are you running here? A petting zoo?" She beat softly on his hip, pulling her punches but letting him know she was angry. "How did you ever manage to get this job? Who hired you anyway?"

"Hired me? Hey, lady, I own the place," he said, draping the net over a grid of wires hung midway between her bed and the ceiling. He wasn't into kinky sex, but if she continued jarring that area of his body, he might have to consider a forbidden pleasure or two. "Watch out."

She stopped whacking his hip and pointed up to him. "You own the Paradise Hotel? Pray tell, what inspired you to get into hotel mismanagement?"

Stepping off the bed, his bare feet touched the floorboards soundlessly, inches from her. His shrug was as big as his smile when he announced, "I won it in a poker game."

Her mouth dropped open.

He *had* won it in a poker game, in the boardroom of Taylor Pharmaceuticals less than ten months ago. Playing against three other unmarried executives, Reilly had won the dubious privilege with aces and queens. As the duly selected undercover man in the field, he would "own" the Paradise Hotel until the bromeliad specimens were safely back at the company's laboratory. Then some other lucky person would take his place. But that information, he reminded himself, was not for Allison

Richards's edification. Nor was the fact that her brother-in-law, Tony Church, had been the botanist hired to gather the specimens.

Closing her mouth, she began nodding her head. "A poker game. That explains a lot."

There she goes again, he thought angrily. Taking aim at his ego with her disapproving, condescending, chin-jutting smile! "Just what does that mean?" he asked evenly.

"It means I'm beginning to understand why you're so anxious to keep silent about Tony."

"And why is that?" he asked, taking a step in her direction. He'd startled her with his movement, and when she stepped back, the lacquered chopsticks in her hair and that irridescent film of a shirt made her look more like a butterfly in flight than a vice president of mortgage loans on a manhunt.

"Because you're evasive, irritating, and irresponsible about everything else around here," she said, flattening her back against the opposite wall.

"You don't know what you're talking about."

"I know exactly what I'm talking about." Sticking out a finger, she tapped him in the center of his chest. "You."

There's a good reason, he wanted to shout as he stared down into those big blue eyes of hers. *I'm saving your brother-in-law's butt and mine by behaving this way.* But he couldn't tell her about the dangerous timber company that would stop at nothing to own this rain forest, and that frustrated him further. "Shut up."

"I will not. You *are* evasive, irresponsible, and irritating. And impolite too."

"Will you shut up?!" he shouted, slamming a flattened hand against the wall behind her.

"Make me."

He accepted the challenge with gusto. Lowering his head, he sealed his lips to hers with a suctioning kiss. The effect was instant and shattering, pulling up a yearning from an untapped depth inside her. Her only struggle was to get closer. Quicker. He was all heat and hands and mouth, filling in the empty spaces of her life in one great surge of masculinity. She grabbed for his shirt sleeves, but instead felt the muscles of his bare arms as they wrapped around her, pulling her close to mold to his will. Her tongue dueled with his. The kiss went on, searching for its place in eternity until someone banged on the door.

Reilly dragged his mouth from hers. "Go

away. Can't you hear us arguing?" he managed before he let her pull him back into the kiss.

"Reilly? Reilly, Puddin' Head came back," Chico said in a loud whisper.

As the child ran back down the veranda, Allison stiffened in Reilly's embrace. He lifted his head, his expression drowsy with desire.

"I'm—I'm appalled at this," she said, not sounding at all convinced.

His eyes hinted at a coming smile as he stroked her jaw with his thumb. "You don't feel appalled," he said, starting back down for another kiss.

Pushing away from him, she wiped his moisture from her lips with a surprisingly shaky hand. "Okay, I'll admit, I was having a dysfunctional moment."

"What a crock," he said, turning his back to the wall to watch her move around the room. "You were functioning just fine, Al."

Reilly, in his indefatigable style, was right. Everything about her was functioning at optimum level. Except her brain. "Not true," she lied. "I let you take advantage of me."

"Really? Was that before or after you pinched my butt?"

"Before." With her voice ringing in her

ears, she knew exactly how she sounded. As if she knew Reilly on an intimate level, and that wasn't true and never would be. Crossing the room, she opened the door. "Just get out."

Shaking his head, he sighed heavily. "You are a piece of work, lady."

She swallowed and started again. "About my brother-in-law. Are you going to tell me where he is?"

"I'll tell you this." He leaned in close to her, trying like hell to ignore the ache in his groin. "I think I was the one having a dysfunctional moment."

"And what is that supposed to mean?" she said, tapping her nails on the open door while she avoided his eyes.

"It means, I don't enjoy having you in my pockets."

"Well, you won't have me in your pockets much longer." Meeting his stare, she followed his eyes as he straightened up. "Coming to this hellhole and laying eyes on you has been a complete waste of my time."

"And mine," he added.

Ignoring his interruption, she continued. "I'm taking the next flight out of here to San Remo."

"I can't wait!" he said, jerking the door from her grasp and slamming it hard after him.

Pulling it open, she stuck her head out. "Neither can I!"

THREE

She was easy to find.

No surprise. With those take-me-to-heaven legs, her impatient attitude, and a command of Spanish that wouldn't get her through Taco Bell, a dead detective could have tracked her down. Reilly still said a prayer of thanks when he found her in the lobby bar of the Hotel de San Remo the following afternoon. He got himself a beer, then started toward her past the bank of potted palms and the cage of squawking parrots.

Intent on the map spread out over her table, she didn't see him coming. That was fine with Reilly. This way he had a few more moments to match his memory with the reality of Allison. At first glance she looked like an advertisement for Barbie Goes Camping with her perfectly tailored khaki shorts outfit, the pink scarf knotted at her neck, and a pith helmet dangling from her chair post. Smiling, he slowed his pace, then stopped completely. She was toying with the end of her French braid, brushing it back and forth against her cheek. How she managed to parlay that innocent gesture into an act of eroticism was beyond him. At least mentally beyond him. Quietly cursing his growing arousal, he pulled on the inseam of his trousers before continuing to her table. Dropping his hat beside her, he waited until she raised her eyes.

"Mind if I sit down?"

The large map she was holding crumpled slightly in her grip. If she was hesitating, it was only to straighten that aristocratic spine another ten degrees. "Yes, I'd mind. I'm expecting someone." With her gaze returning to the map, she reached for his hat and handed it back to him.

Sitting down, Reilly dropped it in his lap and took a swallow of beer. "Who?"

"A tracker named Ramón Quintero, if that's any of your business." Then, apparently annoyed with herself for revealing that much, she folded her arms and looked away. "What do you want, Reilly?"

Ignoring her question, he squinted in exaggerated surprise. "Ramón Quintero?" With a long, low whistle Reilly leaned back, balancing his chair on two legs. "Are you sure you want to hire him? He's a lousy tracker and a worse guide. I heard he lost his last two clients down in Madre de Dios."

Shaking her head, she gave him an indelicate snort. "I told you, my mind's made up." Smoothing the map, she began studying it again. "I'm not leaving until I find Tony, so you can forget trying to scare me away."

Taking a slow breath, he blew it out quietly as he picked at the edges of his beer label. The longer Reilly knew her, the more he realized how determined she was to get to her goal. As determined as he was to get to his. He stared at her, hoping to discover a weak spot in her composure. After a while she checked her watch, then looked toward the door.

"I'm sure you didn't fly down here just to ruin my afternoon. Why don't you get on about your business and I'll get on with mine."

If he'd had any misgivings about his plan, they'd vanished when Allison had mentioned Ramón Quintero. Before Ramón took her money, everyone in the city, including El Diablo Timber, would know about an American botanist named Tony Church wandering around in the rain forest. And Reilly could say good-bye to his carefully tended low profile for Taylor Pharmaceuticals. He hated to think how quickly El Diablo would move its logging operations into that part of the rain forest, ending the chances of it becoming a pharmaceutical-research preserve. And besides all that, Ramón Quintero would take her for a swing in his hammock whether or not she was a willing participant. Dropping the front legs of his chair to the floor, he plunked his beer bottle down and reached for her hand. "Allison?"

Since he'd appeared at her table, every second had been a struggle not to stare at him. It was hard enough fighting back the memory of their kiss while she was breathing in a mix of his clean male scent, his cold beer, and his new cotton shirt. Now he was touching her hand and quietly speaking her name. Her full name. Achy heat was spreading up her thighs when she turned to look at him. "What is it?"

"I came looking for you."

"Why?" *Because you couldn't get that unfinished kissing business out of your mind either? Because you woke up last night throbbing with the need to take it farther, to take me farther?* Swallowing the unvoiced questions, she asked instead,

"Have you heard from Tony? Did he come back to the Paradise Hotel?"

"No. I was thinking over how things got out of hand up there between you and me." He heaved what sounded like a reluctant sigh. "I was wrong and you were right. Tony Church deserves to know he's going to be a father. I know where we can cross paths with him, and if you're still interested, I'll take you to him."

"Oh."

Withdrawing her hand, she tried to dismiss the vague feeling of disappointment. Of course this wasn't about that kiss they'd thrown themselves into or the touchy-feely moments that she had allowed him. This was about something far more important than the pursuit of hot sex. Wasn't it? She eyed him skeptically; something was going on behind those gorgeous green eyes of his. Maybe this was a complete turnaround for Reilly. Maybe he was more responsible than she'd originally thought. Maybe he wasn't. Maybe if she thought about it for one more second, her head would explode.

"Reilly, why would you do this for me?"

"I'm not doing this for you. Tony deserves to know."

She waited for him to blink and revert back to the cocky, confident Reilly Anderson she knew. He was holding a steady gaze while a crazy energy continued building between them. Agitated by her own indecision, she narrowed her eyes at him. "Who's running the Paradise Hotel?"

"Reverend Phillips is doing the cooking. The Bartolino sisters are sharing chambermaid duty in exchange for part of their bill. And Mr. Garfield is off on another Elvis lead."

She wasn't going to comment on his irresponsible behavior concerning his hotel. She had plenty to think about already. "I don't know what to say. First you tell me to go home, and now you're telling me you'll take me to Tony." Shaking her head, she dragged her finger across her lip, then pointed at him. "No, there's something else going on here," she said firmly. "You're not telling me everything."

Reilly squirmed forward in his chair. "Can't a guy just change his mind and admit he was wrong?"

"You'll have to come up with something more convincing that that."

"Like what?"

They both heard someone crying Reilly's name before she could answer. Chico came running through the door, sobbing hysterically and looking frantically in every direction.

When he saw Reilly, he broke into a run across the room and threw himself against Reilly's shoulder. The empty lobby echoed with the Spanish he managed between broken breaths.

Allison was on her feet and around the table instantly. "What is it? What's happened to him?" she asked, pulling the pink scarf from around her neck and shaking it out. She managed to wipe Chico's nose and made a quick pass at his tears before he buried his face against Reilly's chest.

"I brought him down to visit his father and the kid just missed him. Sounds like the timber company he works for sent him to a camp upriver yesterday."

She lifted her head slowly, then backed away. "You flew him down here to visit his father?"

Cursing himself, Reilly patted the boy's shoulder, then brushed the straight black hair away from his eyes. "Yes, but I should have brought him down sooner." Reilly lifted the boy's chin on his finger and spoke soothingly in Spanish.

The words meant little to her, but Reilly's compassionate tone curled around her heart. Soon the boy's heaving sobs quieted to an occasional shudder. She stared down at both of them. "How about a Coke, Chico?" she asked softly.

"He likes it in the can," said Reilly, his eyes never leaving the boy's. "Right, Chico?"

Without turning around, Chico nodded. "I'll open it myself, lady."

She headed for the bar, realizing her challenge had been answered. Reilly's actions with the disappointed child had turned out to be far more convincing than any explanation he could have attempted. When it came right down to it, Reilly Anderson had a heart as big as a teddy bear.

By the time she'd returned from the bar, she had a new plan ready for them. "Reilly, where exactly is this timber camp?"

"Up by Pucalli."

"Is that anywhere near Tony?"

Reilly stared at her for a long time, then nodded. "Yes, it is."

"Great," she said, handing Chico the soda. "If you're serious about taking me to Tony, we can take Chico with us when we go."

"Can we go, Reilly? Can we?" Chico asked, tugging on Reilly's belt and splashing soda on his pants.

"You bet," he said, standing up to inspect the extent of the damage. When he saw it was minimal, he folded the map and dropped it on the table. "Just as soon as we can get you two a couple of backpacks."

"Oh, I won't need a backpack," she said, waving off the suggestion and sitting down. "Everything fits nicely into my suitcases."

"You're only taking what you can carry on your back. Choose wisely. We'll be gone at least a week."

She came off her chair like a bouncing ball. "A week!"

"At least a week," he said, placing her pith helmet on Chico's head. "Let's get going. We have some shopping to do." He tossed a few colorful bills on the table, then headed for the door with Chico in tow.

"But you said you know where he is," she said, picking up her map and purse, then racing to catch up with them. "Why will it take so long to get to him? What's he doing up there?"

"Because we have to take a riverboat. After that, it's deep jungle. And what he's doing up there is his business. By the way, we'll be on foot for a day. Maybe two. Think you'll be able to handle that?" he asked as they stepped into the late-afternoon sunshine.

The magnitude of what she agreed to began sinking in. Up in the jungle with Reilly . . . for days. She hadn't realized she'd stopped walking and had to hurry through the heavy foot traffic along the boulevard. "Of course I can handle it. As long as you don't decide to make it a race," she said crisply.

Since they'd left the capital city two days earlier, Allison had been avoiding him. The closer they got to Pucalli, the quieter she became, spending most of the trip at the boat rail staring at the jungle. Reilly smiled to himself as he watched her making her way along the swaying deck. The sight of her had every one of his muscles tensing with masculine appreciation. She put go-go dancers to shame just trying to keep her balance. He knew by her determined movements forward that she was heading for him. He also knew it by the way she was flaring her nostrils. When she plastered that economy smile on her face, he leaned his elbow on the cargo tarp and waited. Whatever she had to talk about was going to be a pain-in-the-butt subject. But at least she was going to talk.

"Hi," she said too cheerfully, immediately confirming his suspicion.

"'Morning."

Glancing at the caged monkey next to his

shoulder, she asked, "What was the name of the last place we stopped?"

"That was Oca Oca in Paradise Province. This river is the border between Paradise and Oriente. We'll be getting off in Oriente at Pucalli to make arrangements for Chico to meet his father. Then you and I will take a ferry across the river to Paradise." His gaze wandered to her blouse. This was going to be one hell of a trip. He cleared his throat. "Did you sleep okay last night?" *Did you sleep in that lace bra showing so nicely through your blouse?*

"Yes, I did."

Bummer. I would have happily taken it off you . . . slowly . . . with my teeth. He smiled. Maybe he was lousy at flaring his nostrils, but he had other talents. Such as locking his gaze to hers and not letting go until she began to sweat. The problem with that was he ended up sweating too. He turned to slip a piece of fruit through the wire cage by his shoulder. "Where's Chico?"

"Last time I saw him, he was steering the boat," she said, keeping an eye on the tiny arm reaching through the cage. "Tell me again why you made a trip back to the Paradise Hotel for Puddin' Head."

She hadn't left her chair on the sunning

deck to inquire after the monkey, but he'd play along. Hell, he'd do anything to keep her near. Then again, he had all he could do not to pull her into his arms, sniff her hair and taste her all over.

"Puddin' Head's starting to prefer people over his own kind. I decided to take him to new territory after he almost scratched your, uh . . ." Reilly pointed to her breasts, remembering the enticing sensations when he'd delved down between them to search for the fig. His palm was itching to curve around one again. They were perfectly shaped, firm but giving and smooth as warm silk.

"You were going to say 'breasts,'" she said, rimming the underside of her watch with a fingertip. Frowning with the last remnants of indecision, she ran her tongue along the edges of her teeth before she spoke. "Reilly, that's what I wanted to talk to you about. Before we start our trek into the jungle, I think that I should tell you I have no intention of being intimate with you."

"Okay."

"So if you have any plans to—"

"I don't."

"I mean, it's better to settle—"

"It's settled."

She opened her mouth to speak again, then closed it with a quick nod. Turning on her heel, she started back up the deck. He knew he could have suggested she try flexing her knees for better balance, but once she started that marvelous bump and grind he decided against it.

"Al?"

Grabbing the rail, Allison twisted around to face him. Before she could answer, a whistle rudely blasted their arrival into Pucalli. "It's Allison."

"Allison." He tipped his hat and smiled. "I wasn't going to say 'breasts.' I was going to say 'boobs.'"

"I'm surprised you didn't," she said with more bravado than she felt. The boat shuddered to a stop, dropping her center of gravity against the bulkhead. Brushing bits of rust from her shorts, she found her backpack and headed for the gangplank.

His crudeness had actually helped to clear her mind. Until that moment she had agonized over her attraction to him and what their time together could lead to. Plagued with visions of a neatly groomed, impeccably mannered, and irresistibly desirable Reilly guiding her through a tropical paradise, she was afraid she was already seduced. And now this. "Boobs." She shook her head, not caring that several people were staring at her as she muttered the word again.

Two hours later they had crossed the Rio Verde and were standing several yards from its bank. Reilly had pointed out the trailhead twice, but she'd lost it in the tangle of vines and bushes. For one overwhelming moment she wanted to tell Reilly she wasn't going. That it would be better if she stayed at the hotel in Pucalli while he went in there for Tony. She looked across the half-mile-wide river to Pucalli and then at her watch. If they didn't start soon, she was going to lose her nerve completely.

"How's he doing?" she asked, interrupting the spirited conversation in Spanish that Reilly was having with Chico.

Chico answered before Reilly could. "Not good, lady. And it's your fault."

"My fault?" She looked at Reilly. "Why is it my fault that he missed his father again?"

"You tell her, Reilly," Chico said before smearing his tears across his cheeks and walking away.

"He thinks we should all wait in Pucalli

until his father shows up again. That could be three or four days."

"And this is my fault?" she mumbled to Reilly.

"Of course it's not your fault," he said, hooking Puddin' Head's leash to his belt. "Look, I can't leave him in Pucalli and I can't drag him into the jungle either."

"I know that," she said indignantly. She took a step back as the monkey reached out from his perch on Reilly's shoulder. "Maybe I should try talking to him."

"Let me handle this. Man to man."

She rolled her eyes, then tapped her watch. "You said if we get started soon, we can make it to shelter before the afternoon rains begin. You've been handling this for twenty minutes."

"I heard that, lady." Giving her a thoroughly disgusted look, Chico stomped over to her. "Reilly says Pucalli is no place for ladies. He says we gotta take you in the jungle so you can be safe and then later he will bring me back to Pucalli." Wringing his hands and shaking his head, the boy appeared to be on the verge of tears again. "We gonna miss him, Reilly. We gonna miss *mi padre*, and it's her fault."

"Chico, it's not her fault."

Wrenching her shoulders from her back-pack, she dropped it at Reilly's feet. "Woman to boy," she said to Reilly as she grabbed Chico's hand and walked him to the riverbank. She pointed to a dry spot, and when he sat down, she took the place beside him. "I'm going to tell you a story."

Chico looked over his shoulder at a doubt-ful Reilly and shrugged. "Is this gonna take a lotta time, lady?"

"It could," she said, turning the boy's face toward her. "But we have a long walk ahead of us, so I'll give you the short version."

"Hurry up."

"Do you know what a whale is?"

"Yeah, sure," he said, brushing the hair out of his eyes. "I saw one in a book."

"Well, once, when I was your age, I was sailing with my father and a whale crashed into the side of our boat," she said, watching the boy's eyes suddenly rivet to her face and grow bigger. "My sister was screaming. I was crying. The whale kept crashing against the boat. We didn't know what to do, but my father re-minded us that he was the captain and that we had to trust him to do the right thing." She took an enormous breath and let it out slowly.

"We're all alive today because we listened to the captain. Chico, Reilly is our captain."

"Yeah, but what happened to the whale?"

"It's too long a story to tell now. Maybe later when we stop for the rains," she said, walking back to Reilly and the monkey. Chico was on her heels.

"Reilly, come on. Let's go," he said, pointing toward the jungle.

Shrugging into her backpack, she adjusted the weight and looked up at him. "The boy said, 'let's go,' so let's get this show on the road, *bwana*," she said, knowing she was going to savor Reilly's look of surprise for a long time.

"How did you do that?" he asked, still looking dumbfounded while he pointed to Chico. The boy was scurrying over to the trailhead while struggling to put on his backpack.

"I used a business technique that we in the civilized world call negotiating. Something he wanted in exchange for something I wanted. You ought to try it sometime," she said, slipping her hands into her pockets. She smiled modestly. There was nothing quite like a clean kill. They walked wordlessly toward Chico and the trailhead. Her moment of triumph was short-lived when she saw the boy's skeptical expression.

"Lady, that story about the whale better be good," he said before disappearing into the wall of vines and bushes.

Allison winced.

Pushing back a leaf the size of her desk pad, Reilly raised his eyebrows. "The whale?"

Trying to ignore his candy-eating grin, she took her first step into the jungle. She could have kept on walking, but she made the mistake of stopping to look at him. Now was the perfect opportunity for a flippant remark, but she couldn't get the words to come out. And the longer she stared into his eyes, the more breathless she became. Like the exotic jungle palette behind him, every shade of green seemed to be reflected there.

He leaned closer, his voice resonating with unspoken promises. "I'd love to hear that story. Maybe we could negotiate." One side of his mouth curled in a teasing smile. "Something you want for something I want. What do you say?" He winked, and she closed her eyes.

A recalcitrant ten-year-old.

A breast-obsessed monkey.

And a man who made her want to fling

responsibility aside and indulge every one of her fantasies. And then every one of his.

Was it true that God gave you only what you could handle? she wondered. High in the green canopy above, a bird screamed with laughter.

"It's going to be a very long trip."

FOUR

Six hours of racquetball and her worst fears about natural childbirth couldn't possibly compare with the way her body was aching. But catching up with Tony was going to be worth it. She looked up from the ground to see Reilly lounging against a tree waiting for her. They'd been marching uphill for the last thirty minutes, and he still looked like the final frame in a deodorant-soap commercial. With a blister forming on her right heel and her shoulders burning from her straps, she frankly didn't care that she looked like the first frame. Pressing both hands against the tree, she used precious energy to wrinkle her brow and frown. "I thought," she began breathlessly, "that you agreed . . . this wasn't going . . . to be a race."

"It isn't. You insisted we make the trip in one day. Remember?"

"Yeah," she managed before resting her forehead against the back of her hand.

"Hey, you wanna race, lady?" shouted Chico, sprinting by both of them.

While she gasped for breath, she reached out toward the boy. "Reilly, he'll . . . get lost."

"He's fine. He's still revved up from your whale tale, and besides we're just going over this next hill."

"The next hill?"

"Yes," he said, looking her over slowly. He turned abruptly and walked on. "We'd better get out of here before the sun sets, or we could get ourselves into big trouble."

"Reilly. Wait. Please wait," she said, shambling forward to catch him. Her fatigue wound around her like a wet blanket, weighing her down along with the rest of her concerns. "I have to ask you something."

Resting his hand on the shank of his machete, he hesitated turning back to her. He had spent several nights imagining that needy tone directed at him. The trouble was he never imagined feeling guilty when he heard it. "Can't this wait?"

"No. It's about Tony."

"Then ask Tony," he replied, taking a step forward.

"Please, Reilly."

He didn't have a soft, gooey center, but she made him doubt that fact when she touched his elbow. *My elbow, for God's sake.* "Okay. Ask," he said, bracketing his words with a noncommittal shrug. When he turned to face her, she was hooking her thumbs under her pack straps and closing her eyes.

"Is he traveling with a woman?"

"What woman? Oh, you mean is Tony cheating on his wife?"

She kept her eyes closed, her teeth over her bottom lip, and her jaws working from side to side. He ended up dragging her through ten seconds of silence while he tried to imagine what could have provoked the question. In the end he wished he hadn't waited so long to speak, even if he had a right—no, an obligation to keep her away from Tony. In a few more weeks the whole world could benefit from Tony's research. Sure, he had faith in Tony's dedication to the project, but faith was no guarantee that Tony wouldn't take off to be with his wife.

"No, he's not with another woman."

Her sigh practically echoed through the forest.

"Thanks."

Blinking, she pulled her scarf from a belt loop, twisted it, then tied it bandanna style around her head. "I didn't want to think that was possible, but I had to be sure." Clearing her throat, she glanced up at him. "I mean, it would be hard for Susan. She's so emotional."

"Because of the baby?" he asked, watching her striving to be all-business again. She almost made it until he mentioned the baby. Even her quick swallow couldn't wash away the tears thickening her voice.

"She's my little sister, you know. We never thought she'd . . ." Clearing her throat, she tried speaking again. "She's never had to do anything on her own before, and now everything has changed. Once Tony comes to his senses, I know they'll work things out."

Reilly scratched his head as he thought back about his own childhood. Life had thrown his family a few curveballs along the way. He squinted with genuine curiosity. "This loyalty to your sister . . . she must be a very special person."

"Very special," she said, staring hard at her hands. "Susan has had . . . medical problems. We never thought she would be able to get pregnant. This baby is a miracle."

Reilly turned away to give her another moment to gather her emotions and to give himself time to stop feeling like the heel he was. He knew from the beginning that a part of him would regret this decision to keep Allison from Tony. With this new information he realized that he would never have imagined how much. "Ready?"

"Wait." She quickly pressed a knuckle under one eye, then tucked a damp strand of hair under the headband. "Okay. How do I look?"

Soft. Moist. Salty and sweet. Vulnerable. And as much in need of a hug as . . . me. If they didn't move on, he'd start making love to her. "As if you've just walked fifteen miles uphill through a dense tropical rain forest. Let's go." He turned to leave when her nervous little laugh ripped through his heart like a small tornado. Dear God, why hadn't he seen this coming? Of course she was banking everything on seeing Tony in the next few minutes. He rubbed his forehead, then looked up at the thick green canopy of trees. He didn't think he could feel any guiltier.

Then she reached out and touched him.

"Come on, Reilly. I haven't seen my

brother-in-law in months. I don't want to scare him."

He had happily accepted that she could cause a part of him to be hard as rock, but it was the soft spot she'd created in his heart that unnerved him.

"You look fine," he said, taking her by the wrist and pulling her along, "but if we don't hurry, we're going to take a step down on the food chain."

Several minutes later he hacked through a plant stalk with his machete, then pushed the rest of it aside. "Watch your step," he warned, offering his hand. She took it, but before pulling herself forward she pressed her palm to his chest.

"Reilly, I'll never be able to thank you enough for bringing me to him. Maybe when this is all over, we could . . ." Her voice trailed off as she held his head to hers and planted a smacking kiss on his mouth.

In her excitement she ended up stumbling over his boot and landing in a spread-eagle sprawl in the clearing. Laughing, she pushed up and brushed off her chin.

"Tony? Tonyyy? It's me, Allison. Where are you?" Dropping her pack, she scrambled to her feet and ran toward the wooden structure in the center of the clearing. "Where are you, Tony?"

Reilly reached to touch the spot where she'd kissed him, but brought his hand to the back of his neck instead. Damn. There was no perfect solution to this mess, only a perfect opportunity for more regret. And if she yelled, "Surprise!" one more time, he swore he'd fall on his machete.

"No one's here, lady," Chico said from inside the one-room, tin-roofed structure. "Just me and Puddin' Head," he said, pointing to the monkey on the rail.

"Reilly, did you hear that? Tony's not here," she said, twisting around to look at him.

"I heard." He walked up to her with a machete in one hand and her backpack in his other. "Did you get a look at the tree house? We'll be sleeping up there," he said, pointing into the branches of a kapok tree.

The kapok was far taller than any other tree around them. She had to drop her head back and squint through the branches to take in most of it. After an interested search, she gave up. "I don't see any tree house," she said, slightly bewildered. "Where are we? What is this place? Where is Tony?"

"It's an abandoned research station. A German company was here doing some kind of research," he said as he walked over to the half-walled storage pavilion. Reilly had seen to it that the place was stocked once a month for Tony, and by the looks of it his operatives were doing their job. "They left enough food and bottled water to last us for months. And that canoe looks to be in good shape."

Her look of bewilderment grew. "But I thought we were going to a village or a house. You never told me it was so primitive."

"The pizza delivery is a little slow out here." She wasn't laughing, and that was not a good sign. "Well," he said, clapping his hands, "first things first. Let's get settled in before we lose the light."

She followed him up the steps, her words taking on a suspicious edge. "Reilly, where's Tony? Why isn't he here?"

"I don't know." But he did know. He pictured his crackerjack botanist and daddy-to-be surrounded by bromeliads as he worked in that one-man station at the edge of the cloud forest a few more thousand feet up the mountain.

"What do you mean, you don't know?" She took him by the shoulder, and when he wouldn't answer her, she leaned around to face him. Her hands were shaking with barely controlled emotion. "You said you were taking me to him."

"Al, this place isn't a theme park. I can't tell you he's in the third car on the Magic Mountain ride or standing in front of a blue screen pretending to be Mr. Spock. He'll show up." He turned back to checking the boxes and barrels stacked against the walls. Pulling a plastic-webbed cot from a pile, he handed it to her. "Put your arm through this and start climbing the ladder on the kapok tree. I promise you there's a tree house up there. A few hundred square feet of open-air heaven." Turning back to the box he was searching through, he muttered, "Now, where the hell did they put the lanterns?"

The sound of aluminum crashing against the metal edge of the table caused two heads to turn in her direction. When she realized she had their undivided attention, her anger seemed to dissipate, replaced by confusion. "Reilly," she said, narrowing her eyes, "you never said he might not be here. You as much as lied to me. Where is he and what in God's name is he doing out here?"

"I told you, that's not up to me to say. He has his own reasons for being here."

"How long do we have to wait for him?"

"A while."

Her hands went to her hips at the same moment she jutted her chin at him. "What's 'a while' in this part of the world?"

"I guess it's the same as anywhere. Who knows?"

With her next series of actions Reilly finally understood the phrase "coming unglued." She threw up her hands, made a face to frighten a puma, then slammed her hands on the table as Chico scrambled under it.

"This has been a mistake," she shouted. "I'm not spending an extra minute in this over-grown dish garden. I want to go back right now."

"Look, we're all tired. We can talk about this in the morning."

"I want to go now."

Shoving his hands on his hips, he tried staring her down, but then remembered how good she was at that. The next best thing he could think to do was change the subject. "I can't imagine why you'd want to hike back to Pucalli in those sweaty things. And they're still damp from that last rain," he said, giving her clothes a once-over. "Doesn't slipping into that short white nightgown with the lace stuff around here," he said, drawing a half circle low on his own chest, "and snuggling under a mosquito net sound more appealing to you?" He lifted his hands, turning them palms up with a shrug. "It does to me."

Grabbing the cot from the table, she slammed it back into his hands. "You went through my personal belongings without my permission. You are unbelievable. I must have been out of my mind to trust you, you—"

"Sorry, but I didn't want you packing extra weight. By the way, I removed your hair dryer, those red leather shoes with the watchamacallits on the top, all of your—"

She let out a growling scream, momentarily silencing him and the jungle sounds. "Just who do you think you are?"

She turned away for an instant, and Chico took the opportunity to scurry behind Reilly. "Is she gonna throw something?"

"Not a chance. She'd have to sleep on the floor if she did," he said, pressing the cot back into her hands. "And I believe I'm called *bwana*. Now, I suggest you do your part of the chores, or you'll be sitting down here in the dark without a bed, food, or mosquito netting. Alone. Meanwhile," he said, pulling Chico from behind his back, "we'll be cooling off at about eighty feet up there in the canopy because the fruit bats can be rather annoying down here in the understory."

She held his gaze as long as she thought safe, then slipped her arm through the cot and headed for the ladder.

"*Un café?*"

The promising aroma provided the only incentive to move. Her bones ached from yesterday's trip, her throat was scratchy from yelling, and she could have done nicely with another few hours of sleep. She opened one eye. Chico held a cup of coffee under her nose. "Go away."

"I din't think you was gonna wake up," he said, ignoring her plea while he wrapped her fingers around the cup. "You awake now? These 'commodations okay, lady?" asked Chico, sitting next to her on the narrow cot.

Two birds screeched nearby, and a flash of red wings flitted by the railing. Allison blinked and rubbed one eye. "Where did you learn that word?"

"Reilly. He said he think you don't like these 'commodations."

She sipped her coffee, then puckered her lips.

"Pretty good, no? I put four sugars in."

"Thank you," she said, handing it back to him. She dropped her feet to the floor on the opposite side of the bed. Pushing back the mosquito netting, she glanced around the one-room structure. "Where is he?"

"Reilly's at the river making me a . . . I forget the word," Chico said, coming around to her side with a basket of fruit in his arms. "Eat. Reilly says we're goin' swimming when you eat."

"He went back to the Rio Verde?" she mumbled as she rubbed her eyes again. Then it hit her. She was on her feet and starting for the steps. "He left us here?"

"No, lady. He went to this river." He pointed to the far side of the clearing as he pulled her back to the cot. "Down there," he said, indicating a break in the bushes. "You okay, lady? You know how to work the toilet?"

"Yes, those were excellent instructions you gave last night."

"Yeah, but you didn't tip me for that either," he said, sitting down beside her again. "You gonna yell some more today?

"I don't think so." A slow smile started across her lips. "I think I'll apologize. Starting with you," she said, giving him a kiss on the forehead.

He wiped it away and rolled his eyes. "Don't do that, lady," he said, standing and hitching up his shorts. "Eat. Faster." Then he left her, hurrying down the ladder, across the clearing, and into the break in the bushes.

She poured a fresh cup of coffee and sat down to savor the awakening world around her. Alone. Almost alone, she amended, as Puddin' Head dropped onto her cot. She eyed him uneasily. Holding her hand to her breastbone, she tossed him a fig from the basket and inched away from him. She had other things to worry about besides a nervous monkey. In a few minutes she was going down to the river and humble herself in front of Reilly. As angry as she had been last night and as much as Reilly deserved her wrath, he was going to get an apology. He deserved it because she'd overreacted. Because it was the right thing to do. She stared into her cup. And because he'd never tell her another thing about Tony if she didn't.

Twenty minutes later she stood at the riverbank watching Reilly and the boy. Waist deep in the water, Reilly was pulling Chico around on an anchored bamboo raft. He looked like a glistening river god cavorting with his worshipful subject, and his laughter was a bright note blending with the other sounds in the rain forest. She thought she'd caught her smile in time, but it was already breaking across her face. Tarzan had returned, announcing his arrival with a quiver of recognition deep in her belly.

The sight of his unbound hair, wet and curling near his shoulders, was already doing its deed. Why did he have to be so heartstoppingly handsome that it made her forget to breathe? The sun reflecting off the river made him gleam with gold light. Exhaling in one long sigh, she reminded herself that she hadn't flown nine hundred miles to fulfill her Tarzan fantasies. Even if those fantasies were taking on more adult themes.

"Hello."

Knowing she couldn't trust her voice, she answered him with a wave. In a moment more, she told herself, she'd have this silly fantasy in its place. He was waving back when his playful expression began to change. He started sinking lower in the water, then disappeared beneath the surface. Several seconds drifted by. She took a step closer to the water. If Reilly thought he was being funny, he wasn't.

"Chico?" Pulling off her shoes, she threw them behind her. "What's he doing? Can you see him?"

Chico didn't answer. The boy continued staring at the place Reilly had been. Fear, like a dozen sharp pins, began pricking her in the heart. This couldn't be happening; he couldn't be gone. "Reilly? Reilly?" She'd made it into thigh-deep water when he burst through the surface.

"BLAAAAGHHHH!!"

His shout vibrated through her like a blast from the riverboat whistle. Too relieved to scold him, she stood in place as he lunged toward her.

"Pretty good trick, lady. No? We scared you good," Chico said between fits of laughter.

Avoiding Reilly's stare was the real trick. "You scared me good," she conceded, dropping her glance. The edges of her shorts were soaking up water, and she began rolling them higher.

Dragging his hand down his face, Reilly wiped the water from his eyes and started toward her again. He'd never seen a banker with thighs like those. Satin smooth, firm, and damn sexy with water purling around them.

And if she didn't stop touching them, he'd have to dive for deep water.

"She's very brave, Chico."

"Reilly, she's not brave. She's a girl."

"Of course she's brave," he said, watching her downcast eyes growing wider with each of his advancing steps. "She rushed into the river without asking how safe it is."

Her stare broke up into darting glances around them.

"There's nothing dangerous in this water, is there?" She stiffened, then started toppling forward. Both of her hands hit him at the same moment, then began sliding down his chest.

"Besides you?" he asked, catching her as they both slipped. She struggled to move away from him as heaven began exploding on his skin again. Soft, fair pieces of it in the form of her hands and breasts. Hips and thighs. And once, her mouth. How, he wondered, could she send fire racing through his veins while they were struggling to keep their heads above water?

She managed to make it up on her feet, then took two careful steps backward. "No more joking, you two," she said, looking down at her wet clothes.

What she'd done to him was no laughing matter. "No more joking," Reilly agreed quietly, sinking into the water to hide his arousal. By the attention she was paying to her own clothes, he was fairly certain she wasn't aware of his state.

Starting for the shore, she slowed to a stop as a leaf floated toward her. For a long while she stared at it, then looked up at the trees before turning back to Reilly.

"This was how I used to picture it."

"Picture what?" he asked, watching her soft expression.

"Tarzan and the jungle. Everything light and fun and easy." She pressed back a lock of her hair and stared down at him. "You know. No responsibilities, no worries. Just the pleasures of paradise and all the time in the world to enjoy them. It all seemed so possible . . . when we were children." Lifting her arms partway into the air, she turned completely around. "Oh, I used to dream about this." Her wistful gaze drifted to Chico, then back to Reilly. "I could almost believe . . . " shaking her head, she turned to go.

He'd seen that shimmering look once or twice before, but this time was different. This time she'd put a name to it. So Ms. Allison Richards of the mortgage loan department, wearer of linen suits, protectress of her pregnant sister, and possessor of a body to kill for, had a thing for Tarzan. His own imagination went into overdrive.

"Wait up," he said, coming out of the water. Splashing into the shallows, he stopped between her and the riverbank. He wanted another peek behind those China-blue eyes, another moment to hear her talk, another chance to touch her. Tugging at her hand, he gently turned her around. "How about a swim?"

She laughed a short, embarrassed laugh that lit him up inside. It was a quiet laugh that he could swear she'd been saving for him. A soft sound that in the right circumstance could be urged into a whisper. And maybe even a moan.

"I didn't come down here to swim. I came to apologize for losing my temper last night." She picked her wet blouse away from her skin. "Even though I was tired and disappointed, I shouldn't have exploded like that." Lifting her face a little closer to his, she whispered, "I'm sorry."

Without realizing it, he was pulling her closer.

"You gonna kiss him, too, lady?"

She backed away instantly. "No more jokes," she said, shaking a finger at Chico.

Without meeting Reilly's eyes, she ducked away toward the shore. "I'd better change into something dry and hang up these clothes.

Opening up to him was getting to be a habit that she'd have to break. True, he hadn't brought up yesterday's impulsive kiss or her Tarzan nonsense the rest of the morning, but she couldn't shake the feeling that he was setting her up for something. She'd bet her plane ticket to Costa Rica that there was much more to Reilly Anderson than met the eye. She caught him staring at her during lunch, and when their knees bumped under the table, he gave her an odd smile. After lunch while Reilly appeared to be relaxing in the hammock, she could sense the wheels turning in his head. Once, when he was on the floor playing with Chico and Puddin' Head, he looked at her in a way that made her forget her suspicions. His searching look took her back to those revealing moments in the river with him. She finally had to look away. Maybe it was time to slow down the wheels in her own head. Somewhere behind the candy-eating grin and well-worn clothing was a story that she was getting desperate to hear.

When Reilly and Chico found a soccer ball and took it into the clearing to play, she took the opportunity to see if her clothing was dry. She'd hung her things over a wooden crate behind the storage pavilion. Her shorts and blouse were where she'd left them, but her underwear was missing. Nothing to panic over, she told herself as she checked the surrounding area. Down on her hands and knees, she looked around the four-foot stilts supporting the building. Nothing. Not a sign. Pushing up from the ground, she wondered what could have happened to it? Who in the world . . . ? Her last thought brought her to attention. Good thing, she told herself, that she hadn't bet her plane ticket to Costa Rica. The jerk. Walking out in the clearing and up to Reilly, she stood in front of him, preventing him from putting the ball in play.

"This move is too juvenile, even for you, Reilly."

He tossed the ball in the air, bounced it off his knee, and caught it. "Haven't you heard? The Uruguayans perfected this move."

"You know what I'm talking about." Wiggling the fingers of her outstretched hand, she warned, "You'd better hand—"

"You think I'd give up this ball that easily?"

he asked, maneuvering around her to kick the ball toward Chico. "We're talking soccer here, dear."

"We're talking panty raid. It was a matched set, pink, and I'd like it back."

He squinted at her, oblivious to the soccer ball whizzing by his head. "What the hell are you talking about?"

"You're going to make me say it, aren't you." Shaking her head, she folded her arms and stared at his ear. "My underwear. Panties and bra." She tapped her foot. "Well, don't just stand there. Say something."

He rubbed his mouth, nodding as his brow furrowed in concentration. "Pink?"

"Pink."

"What shade of pink?"

"Sort of shell pink with a white pinstripe running thr—" The moment she realized he'd set her up, she felt a growl gather in her chest and erupt, mid-sentence, into a full-blown scream. The man was going to be the death of her, but she was going to take him with her when she went.

"Hey, lady, you said you wasn't gonna yell today."

FIVE

"Why would I take your underwear?"

"I don't know. I don't want to know. I just want them back. Immediately."

"Okay, okay. We'll get them back." Reilly turned to the boy. "Do you know where her underwear is?"

"No, Reilly," he said, solemnly shaking his head.

Sliding her arm around the boy's shoulder, Allison ruffled his hair. "I didn't think you had them, Chico."

Chico sighed with resignation. "Thanks, lady. Just don't kiss me."

"As for you," she said, flaring her nostrils at Reilly, "I'm not so sure." Gathering her dignity, she headed for the ladder.

She had placed her foot on the first rung

when Reilly said matter-of-factly, "You shouldn't be wearing underwear anyway."

Twisting in midair in one smooth movement, she managed a giant stride onto the ground toward Reilly. "What is wrong with you?" she asked in a hiss as she reached for Chico and covered his ears with her hands. "Don't you have any concern for the moral upbringing of this child?"

Chico pulled her hands away. "Hey, lady. Don't worry. I don't wear no underwear too. And Reilly don't no more." He shrugged in childish disbelief. "Nobody wears that stuff. Only *los gringos*."

Reilly's eyebrows lifted. "The kid's right. I hesitated telling you because I knew you'd balk at the idea. It's a practical matter, Al. If you insist on wearing underwear, you have a fifty-fifty chance of developing a rash in some out-of-the-way places. You see, because of the constant humidity, you need as much air as possible circulating around—"

"Okay, okay. I get the idea," she said, holding up her hands."

"Just in time. You're down to your last set of undies." Twirling his finger in the general direction of her body, he continued. "Those pale blue ones with the tiny white flowers all over them."

She felt her eyes opening wider, but she was too shocked to speak.

"When I took out your hair dryer, I removed some other unnecessary items from your pack and replaced them with first-aid material. You'll find bandages and antifungal ointment down near the —"

Her hand sliced through the air between them, cutting him off. "I want my underwear!"

With a more elegant flourish of his hand he stepped back and bowed. "Take us to the scene of the crime."

"I'm not goin'," Chico announced as he walked off toward the bushes. "I gotta find the ball."

Pretending to neaten a nonexistent tie, Reilly straightened up. "Let's begin at the beginning. Where did you leave them?"

"You know they were on a crate back there."

"I swear, I didn't know that."

"If you're lying . . ." She watched his brow wrinkle with surprise. Was it possible he didn't know where the missing underwear was? Not likely, since he described the set she was wearing. Not likely, but by the way he was waiting for her to move, still possible. Heading for the area behind the pavilion, she jerked her thumb toward the weathered boards. "I checked in there, I checked behind the pilings, I even checked the bushes. They're gone, Reilly, and I am not amused." She stopped long enough to get a glance at his face as he passed her. "Why are you laughing?"

"I feel like telling you to calm down and keep your pants on, but somehow that doesn't seem appropriate," he said before heading around the back corner. He started down to the ground, but before his knees touched the leafy covering, Allison hauled him up.

"That's it! I've had it," she said, bunching the front of his T-shirt in both her fists. She leaned in close to him, enunciating each word. "I don't want you cracking any more jokes at my expense." Jerking up his shirt in her fury, she leaned closer. "I don't want you touching my personal belongings." Twisting the material, she managed to deliver a thump to his chest with each syllable. "And I don't want you—"

"Oh, yes you do. And I want you," he said firmly as his arms banded around her back. Without warning he pulled her hips hard against him, then brought his face closer to hers. "I want you, Allison. Do you hear me? All that fire in your eyes isn't anger. Whether you want to admit it or not, it's passion. Hot and heavy, singing out to me. And every inch of me is hearing you." He gave her a little shake. "We want each other. Like cats want cream."

"Cream . . . ?" Her mouth dropped open, then closed enough to form a sentence. "Why, you arrogant son of a —"

Before she got the last word out, he brought her face to his, silencing her with a long and stolen kiss. He asked for the next with a tender whisper of her name. That kiss and more were already his. When she eased into his embrace, he slipped his knee between hers and leaned her against the corner piling.

"Maybe more than cream," he said, coming down on her mouth again. Bracing one of his hands on the floorboard next to her shoulder, he looked at her through half-closed eyes. "Maybe a lot more."

He nibbled. He nudged. He nuzzled his mouth against hers, making it slick with his moisture and pouty with need.

"Maybe," she murmured, tugging the elastic from his hair and sinking her fingers into the gold-tipped mane. Opening her mouth, she welcomed his probing tongue with a lick from her own.

Chico's laughter rang out from the other side of the pavilion. As they heard him running up the steps and across the floorboards, Reilly reluctantly backed out of her arms. His intimate stare continued as the sound of the boy's laughter and the vibration of his footsteps drew closer.

Nervously smoothing her hair, she tried to pull her gaze from his, but Reilly's command of the moment was still overwhelming her senses. She *had* to look at him. "Why are you staring at me like that?"

"Why do you think?" he asked, drawing a thumb across her lip, then sucking the moisture from its pad. "Soon. I promise," he whispered before they looked up to see Chico inside the building.

"Reilly! Look! Look!" Chico, hugging a soccer ball and bouncing on his toes, pointed to the trees behind the pavilion.

She had barely gotten a good lungful of air, when Reilly carefully pointed out her bra to her. It was at least forty feet up in the kapok. She overlooked it at first, thinking the delicate pink twosome was a pair of orchids, side by side. Then she noticed the straps. On the same branch Puddin' Head was frantically tugging on a snagged pair of shell-pink panties. The tiny animal suddenly slipped, catching himself in a leg opening. Swaying and screeching, he bared his teeth in disapproval.

"It *wasn't* you. Reilly, y-you didn't take them," Allison said before sliding to her haunches in breathless laughter.

They were all laughing as they watched Puddin' Head's face appear, then disappear through one leg opening while his tail dangled out of the other. When Allison could trust her voice again, she glanced up at Reilly, then back to the monkey. "You were right about things not being safe sitting around out here."

"Next time nail your wet clothing to the rail," Reilly said through the last of his laughter.

Wiping away a giddy tear, she kept on staring at the monkey. "Well, I guess it's time for another apology."

"No need," he said, allowing Chico, who was straddling the rail, to climb down onto his shoulders. Clasping his hands around the boy's ankles, he started away from her. "I'd say everything worked out." A second later he came back into her view. "To a point," he added before disappearing around the corner with a lazy grin.

She grinned back, then shook her head in disbelief. Just when she thought she could write him off, he had to go and do this to her! Touching her lips, she tried to bring back that moment when he'd stroked them with his thumb. The thought of his touch had her sizzling with desire. What an incredibly thorough lover he must be. And what an impossible fantasy that was, because she wasn't going to be his lover. Ever.

Scrambling to her feet, she fought for control of her runaway thoughts, attempting to tame them with a reasoning mind. So what if she'd discovered a match for his passion within herself? She couldn't pretend the rest of her well-ordered life back in Connecticut didn't exist. It didn't matter that he kissed like a wild man—with his lips and tongue and body, and somehow, she knew, with his heart. She didn't need him introducing new . . . things to her.

Flipping up the collar of her blouse, she began pacing like a caged cat. Things. What in heaven's name would she do with these things, or worse, the memories of them when she was back in her real life? *Things.* She didn't even have a name for what he would do to her. For what she wanted him to do to her. Her skin tingled when she remembered how he'd surged against her with desire potent enough to take her breath away.

She kicked the piling, then turned to lean on it again. Damn him and his sensual onslaught. She had lived a full life before meeting him. Hadn't she? At least a mature, responsible adult kind of life. Hell, even if it was half a life, she was an intelligent, sensible, take-charge person who would get right to work on filling up the empty half with acceptable . . . things. Yes, that was it. There was Susan's baby, her career at the bank, a planned vacation now and then. And plenty of men without ponytails and promises and plans to make her toes curl.

A yellow-headed parrot flashing its scarlet wings and sending out its gravelly call brought her out of her problems and back to Paradise. In the distance she heard Reilly attempt to match the bird sound.

Reilly Anderson might have discovered this wanting, needing part of her, but that didn't mean she would allow him to explore it. His irresponsible, unambitious, devil-may-care lifestyle would never mesh with hers, even if she was still having fantasies about him at ninety. She knew so little about Reilly . . . but that little was still too much.

Heading back to the main area of the clearing, she found the two of them sitting on the front steps of the pavilion, their heads cocked and their eyes slightly unfocused. Evidence of their soccer game remained in the form of mud on their toes, knees, and forearms.

Another bird sent out its whooping call through the trees.

Reilly nodded. "Got it. We'll try it like this," he said, holding his crooked fingers to his lips. After two failed attempts to replicate the sound he let loose with the whooping bird call. Several seconds later the sound returned from the interlocking branches beyond the clearing.

Allison watched as Chico attempted to reproduce the sound. The result was disappointing, but Reilly patiently demonstrated the correct placement of his fingers again.

"Watch your thumb. That's the way."

When Chico managed a squeaky but recognizable version, they both cheered the accomplishment.

"Hey, lady, you like that?" Chico asked when he noticed her standing nearby.

She smiled in acknowledgment. The two could have been father and son or mentor and student, but the term *kindred spirit* seemed to fit them best of all. When Reilly and the boy attempted a duet, the moment turned to pure enchantment. Afterward Reilly patted the space next to them.

"Come on. Dr. Anderson's School of Jungle-Bird Calls is taking new students."

"Yeah, lady. Reilly will teach you good."

With all her complaints about him, there remained one unarguable fact. Under his rakish trappings Reilly Anderson was a decent man; there wasn't a mean bone in that magnificent body. Closing her eyes for an instant, she reminded herself that she didn't need more praiseworthy facts about Reilly to confuse her. What she knew about him firsthand was already confusing enough. Clearing her throat, she announced, "No, thank you. I'm going down to the river."

"We'll keep you company," Reilly said, pushing up from the step.

Puddin' Head dropped to the floor where Reilly had been, protesting the big man's move with a throaty yowl. Reilly bent down, allowing the monkey to scamper up his arm and onto his shoulder. Two chunks of mud dropped from Reilly's elbow as he stood. A moment later a chunk of mud fell from Chico's knee. The two looked slowly down to the ground and then at each other.

"If you'll have us," Reilly concluded with a tempting grin.

The harmony of the moment dissolved into a cacophony of jungle screeches. The unexpected noise brought Allison out of her trance-like state. Back in the real world this was Wednesday. Pulling several hairpins from her hair, she began neatening her straggling top-knot. She had loan reviews on Wednesday. She picked up her dry cleaning on Wednesday. She had her nails done on Wednesday. One hairpin remained in her hand, and bringing it down in front of her, she twisted it into several different patterns. When she attempted to return it to its original shape, she realized the pin would never be the same. Shoving it into her pocket, she reminded herself that she should be in Connecticut or at that four-star resort in Costa Rica. Whichever place she belonged, it wasn't here. She shouldn't be here. And she shouldn't be loving this silly, crazy moment. But she was here and she was loving it. Heart and head. Body and soul.

"That's okay, guys. I need some time by myself." Time to get her head on straight again. Time to reason a way out of this sensual time warp that Reilly kept wedging into her life.

With the world spinning around her in vivid scents and exotic sounds, Allison ran blindly for the river. All of her senses were teasing her, tempting her to turn back toward Reilly. Halfway between Reilly and the river she stopped. Broad leaves and tickling ferns settled against her body, and then the rain began. Pattering drops that quickly turned into a downpour. Trapped. She was trapped in this emerald-hued paradise, and she had to get out before it ate her alive.

The next morning while Chico was retrieving her underwear, Allison stood watching beside Reilly in the tree house. They were eighty feet above the floor of the rain forest, and cool breezes were wafting through the sun-filled room. The first night she'd slept up here, she was too exhausted to think about Reilly being a reach away. Last night she couldn't take her mind or her eyes off him. While sleep eluded her, her common sense hadn't. She had finally reached the conclusion that once back in Pucalli, she was going to offer Reilly double whatever he charged her to come back out here to wait for Tony. Alone. Meanwhile she would wait in Pucalli.

"Atta boy," Reilly shouted down through the branches. "To your left. That's good."

Allison winced as the barefoot boy inched through the leaves along the branch. Balling her hands into fists, she bit off a scream when Chico's foot slipped. "If he were my son," she began.

Reilly turned and leaned an elbow on the half wall. "Why don't you have a little boy?"

"That's . . . personal." About as personal as him knowing her brand of underwear or the wanton way she responded to his mouth and hands. "I-I still have time," she stammered. "I'm only twenty-seven."

"Twenty-seven?" he repeated, kinking one eyebrow.

"Yes, twenty-seven." Hot blood rushed to her face, stinging her cheeks and forcing her eyes open wider. Since the moment they'd met, he'd made a game of shocking her. She'd proudly held her own with him in that regard. Until this time. *Why this time?* "I'd ask the same of you, but I think I know the answer."

He rubbed his chin as if he had a beard growing there. Funny, she thought, for all his bad habits, Reilly managed to shave twice a day. Where in the world had he picked up that gentlemanly habit?

"You think you know the answer? And what's that?"

"Please don't take that wrong. You're awfully good with Chico, but you don't seem the domestic type."

Reilly's laughter rumbled quietly through his chest. "Al, that's the nicest thing you've ever said."

She studied his puzzling smile but decided not to pursue the issue. The less she knew about the intriguing man, the less she would have to forget. Besides, she needed other questions answered. "Reilly, how dangerous is Pucalli?"

"Dangerous enough that I'd never consider leaving Chico with anyone but his father."

"Hey, lady. Look. I got 'em."

Reilly sent the boy a victory salute as he watched Chico shimmy back along the limb. "Just look at him, Al. They'd have to lock him in a room to keep him out of trouble in that town."

"He's a little boy. Who would hurt him?"

"Pucalli sprang up overnight. It's filled with some nasty characters. Timber bosses. Greedy people." He gave her a questioning frown. "What's with all these questions about Pucalli?"

"This part of the trip hasn't been working out the way I expected. And, well . . . once we're back there, I've decided to stay and wait in Pucalli for Tony."

"Once *we're* back there?"

She nodded, suddenly uncomfortable under his scrutinizing gaze. "I'll pay you double to come back for Tony and bring him to me."

"But you're not going to Pucalli with me."

"What? Of course I am," she said with a laugh. "You didn't think I'd stay out here by myself while you take Chico to his father, did you?"

"Let's back up. Why did you come to San Rafael?"

"To find my brother-in-law, but—"

"Well, you can forget about finding him if you leave now. He's going to show up anytime, and if someone isn't here, he'll go off again." *And if I take you to Pucalli, you'll have it spread all over town that Tony Church, botanist extraordinaire, is out here.*

"I'll leave a note for him."

"That won't work. In order for Tony to find it, you'd have to hang it in plain sight. Kind of like your underwear. If Puddin' Head doesn't take off with it, then one of his curious cousins will." As if on cue, a howler monkey growled close by.

"But surely you don't mean for me to stay out here alone?"

He shrugged. "We'll miss him if we both go. This is your last chance, Allison. If you don't catch him in the next few days, you might as well forget meeting up with him."

Never in a dozen lifetimes could she have foreseen this dilemma coming. "There must be some way we can work this out."

Patting her on both shoulders, he looked her squarely in the eyes, giving her a buck-up smile. "This could be a lot more fun than a foray into someone's credit history."

She shrugged off his touch, then crossed her arms tightly over her middle. He could smell her fear, but leaving her here overnight was a safe choice. There were no pumas, no poisonous snakes, and if she used her mosquito netting and left off her underwear, not an inch of that gorgeous body would be marred.

"Don't you owe it to your sister?" he asked softly.

"What do you know about what I *owe* Susan?" she asked, slapping a hand to her chest.

"Well, pardon me, Miss Richards, but while you're treating me like a nosey neighbor, I'm trying to figure out what your problem is." Picking up his backpack, he dropped it on the table and unzipped the side pocket. "So what is your problem?"

"I'm scared, dammit!" she snapped.

"Scared I'll leave you out here all alone? Scared I won't come back?" he dropped his voice to a husky whisper. "Or scared I'll stay?"

"A few accidental kisses and you think I couldn't control myself with you? That's ridiculous," she said, straightening her arms to him.

"Is it? Last night after Chico fell asleep, I invited you to go down to the river with me. You were quick to say no. And even quicker to work up a good yawn, but you and I both know you weren't tired."

"I *was* tired," she said, backing up a step when he moved toward her.

The side of his neck brushed her face when he reached behind her. She heard the flashlight fall over on the shelf, and when he reached for it again, she grabbed his belt to keep from falling. She stumbled backward anyway, and he caught her with one arm. His face came kissably close to hers.

"You couldn't have been that tired. You

were tossing on your cot until three o'clock this morning."

"So were you."

She breathed in his scent, a mix of soap and warm, masculine skin. How delicious it would be to give in to the urge to taste him right now. To fit her tongue over the curve of his Adam's apple. To press long, wet kisses along his jaw. Her legs quivered to fall open for more of his weight. His slow smile was mesmerizing.

"Why couldn't you sleep?" she asked, vaguely aware that she was losing a battle and not caring.

"Because every time I closed my eyes, I kept seeing you naked with a can of Reddi Whip in your hands."

Before she could do anything but swallow, he pulled her up straight and stepped away from her. "I guarantee you'll be safe here until I get back. After that it's every man for himself."

Chico leaped from a branch and landed on the floor of the tree house. Puddin' Head sailed in after him.

Picking up the leash, Reilly fastened it to Puddin' Head's collar, then handed a fig to him. The monkey scurried under the table.

"Hey, lady," said Chico as he tossed Allison's

underwear onto the table. Patting it with his hand, he shook his head. "Did you pay lotsa money for this?"

"What?" she asked, finally coming out of the sensual haze Reilly had her in.

"Lady, I seen cobwebs thicker than this stuff."

"Forget about cobwebs," Reilly said, hooking Puddin' Head's leash to the table leg. "We're leaving for Pucalli in half an hour."

For the next thirty minutes Reilly went over everything Allison needed to know. The more he talked, the more she appeared to relax with the idea of spending the night alone. She caught on quickly, brushing aside his offers to repeat instructions. *Where were you*, he thought, *when I was reorganizing Taylor Pharmaceutical's marketing division?*

"Don't kiss me, lady," Chico said, fending her off with both hands a short time later. "You can shake my hand."

"Take care," she said, stealing a squeeze, "and have a good visit with your father."

"Keep Puddin' Head tied up for a few hours. I don't want him following us to Pucalli."

Allison eyed the creature warily. "Are you sure you don't want to take him with you?"

"They'll put him in a stew there," he said,

shrugging into his backpack. "I should see you tomorrow afternoon." Smiling, he extended his hand toward her.

She took it, but as soon as Chico began descending the ladder, Reilly pulled her close. His eyes locked with hers, and a shiver of anticipation zipped up her spine. But when she thought he was going to kiss her, he whispered last-minute instructions in her ear instead.

"Let down your hair. Shake up the monkeys. And get rid of these things before I get back," he said, holding up her underwear with his free hand.

Reilly made it down the ladder and across the clearing before he turned back for a wave. "Don't worry about a thing. You'll be fine. There's a gun in the box under the water bottles," he shouted before disappearing into the forest.

Two days later Reilly walked into the clearing and looked up to the tree house. "Luuuuucyyyyy! I'm ho-oome!"

"Reilly? Reilly, is that you?" Allison shouted. She was out of the tree house and climbing down the ladder as quickly as she could manage. "Oh, Reilly," she cried, meeting him partway. "I thought something terrible had happened to you and Chico. All sorts of horrible things ran through my mind. You were gone two days. Two nights. What happened? What took you so—?"

He dropped his pack in the dirt and pulled her into his arms, silencing her rush of words with a solid kiss. "Missed me, did you?" he asked when he finally came up for air.

"I was worried about you," she said, looking up at him through her lashes. "All right, yes. I missed you."

He was in a quandary as to what to do next. Kiss her again or drink her in with his gaze. Since he had her in his arms and pressed against his body, he decided that looking would do for the time being. She hadn't let down her hair as he had suggested, but she was wearing it in a crown-high tail. By the soft feel of her breasts, he happily surmised she'd gotten rid of her bra. He'd check on the panties later. "No major events?"

"Puddin' Head ran off last night. I haven't seen him—"

Pulling away, she started again. "Reilly, where were you? What kept you away a second night?"

Before he could answer, a smattering of

raindrops turned into a gully-washing downpour. Reilly grabbed his backpack and Allison's hand, then headed for the pavilion. When he'd dropped his pack on the floor and wiped the rain from his face, he reached for Allison, filling his arms with her.

"By dinnertime last night I was worried sick about you, Reilly. Did something happen to Chico? Was his father late again?"

"Nothing so dreadful," he said with an easy grin. "As it happened, I got myself into a poker game that lasted longer than expected."

He watched her start that blinking thing she did right before she screamed. Unfortunately he couldn't tell her he had had a difficult time rounding up his operatives. "Now, hold on. There's a very good explanation for why I was playing cards."

Pushing him away, she said quietly, "Don't tell me. You've won yourself another hotel, and now you're considering opening up a chain of them. Congratulations, you bastard."

She didn't scream. She didn't speak. Turning away from him, she headed down the steps and into the rain.

SIX

"Hey, what happened to my happy camper?" Reilly asked, following her to the edge of the steps. "Allison? Where do you think you're going?"

"None of your business."

"You'll get soaked."

"But I'll get away from you," she shouted, making her way across the clearing.

Reilly watched the mud splatter, then wash away on her shapely calves as she kept on marching. Slowly shaking his head, his gaze moved up her body. His British friends would have said her knickers were in a twist, but the smooth curves of her backside told him she wasn't wearing knickers. He let out a short, sharp grunt of masculine appreciation.

She stopped once as Puddin' Head scampered up to her. When she stepped over the little monkey, he screamed at her, then dropped on all fours and headed for cover.

If Puddin' Head knew enough to come in out of the rain, then Allison should be heading back any second, Reilly reasoned. He squinted through the pearly sheets for a sign that he was right. Her rigid posture never faltered, even when she made several inelegant slides in the mud. Raising his hands, he cupped them around his mouth. "There's not a dry spot between here and the Rio Verde," he shouted. Reilly tapped his fingers on a roof support. If she didn't stop soon, she'd be into the jungle.

At last his efforts were going to be rewarded; she was turning around and she was . . . flipping him the finger! Passing his hand over his drying shirt and frowning, he started down the steps and into the rain.

The moment she saw him move, she picked up her pace, disappearing into the leafy green wall. Calling her name, he sprinted after her, cursing loudly. There was a limit to his patience. When he found her, she was breaking a broad leaf from a gunnera plant and raising it over her head to shelter herself from the rain. He took her by the arm and turned her around. "Where do you think you're going?"

"Back to Pucalli." Jerking her arm from him, she flopped the leaf over her head and started out again.

"You'll never make it."

"The hell I won't."

He caught up with her again, turning her around with more force this time. "What's it going to take to stop you?"

"Not you," she said, glaring up at him from beneath the three-foot leaf. The rain was spiking his lashes, dribbling off his nose and chin, and straightening the dark hair on his chest. She tried telling herself he was pathetic with his hair plastered to the sides of his neck and his unbuttoned shirt looking like a second skin as it defined his hardened nipples and each muscle of his torso. She swallowed. That rippling, tanned torso that disappeared at his waist into khaki lightweights was anything but pathetic. "Not you," she said again, shaking her head. Too late she realized the words were spoken more to herself than to him.

Cursing, he pulled the leaf umbrella from her hands and threw it into a fern bank. "Yes, me," he said, picking her up and tossing her onto his shoulder. "Don't wiggle, or, I swear, I'll take a swat at this fanny!"

His shoulder whooshed the air from her

lungs with each step out of the jungle and through the clearing. Allison dropped her face onto his back with a disbelieving sigh. Dragged back to his lair as if she were a wounded animal. This would be the end of life as she knew it. Sort of. She gave up struggling and spent her energy on stopping her braless breasts from jiggling against his back. It was no use. She and Reilly were about as familiar with each other's bodies as two about-to-be lovers could be.

"What was that groan for?" he asked, stepping over a buttressed root and standing her in front of the tree-house ladder. Thick lower branches offered a partial respite from the rain.

"Don't ask." She tried pushing him to one side, but he'd staked his position and wasn't budging. "And would you please get out of my way."

Sidestepping her, he made himself into a human wall by jamming his fists to his hips. "You're not going anywhere in this rain."

"Fine. I'll wait in the pavilion until it's over."

He pointed up the ladder. "Up," he said, jutting his chin toward the tree house.

"Why? Haven't you had enough fun with me today?"

"Hell, no."

The rain wasn't quitting, and neither was Reilly. If she went up in the tree house now, at least she would have a chance to pack a few things before starting out for Pucalli. Taking her time, she squeezed the rain out of her ponytail and removed the tie that held it. With a huffy sigh she turned her back to him and climbed the ladder. Reilly followed her after retrieving his pack. Once inside he tossed it in a corner and began stripping off his shirt.

"I'm starved," he said, toeing off one boot, then starting on the other. "Let's send out for Chinese."

"I've got a better idea," she said, pulling off her wet sneakers and throwing them at him. He tried dodging them, but she hit him both times on the legs. "Why don't we send *you* out for it?"

In the confines of the tree house she had a choice of two things to look at. The rain-soaked, pearly shades of green outside or a bare-chested Reilly. She chose Reilly. Shirtless, and with his hair falling in thin, curling spears against his chin, he looked as if he'd stepped out of an action-adventure movie. His shoulders were certainly broad enough and his arms perfectly muscled and corded to fight off any enemy. Or hold any heroine. An image of him carrying her through the jungle suddenly appeared in her mind. A shirtless Reilly wearing those khaki and belted trousers and mid-calf bushmaster boots.

Or maybe just a loincloth. And a smile.

Gritting her teeth, she closed her eyes, telling herself she was suffering temporary insanity. "You left me out here so that you could gamble. How could you be that inconsiderate?"

"Hey, that was a very important poker game," he said, taking several blankets and arranging them in a pallet on the floor.

His answer would have been bad enough if he'd delivered it with humor, but his sober expression was more than she could bear. Reilly Anderson was an incorrigible adolescent with no chance of redemption, and she was a fool to stay a moment longer. And mad to say another word to him. "I missed you, dammit!"

He looked up at her. "I knew you would."

The sound of the rain blended with the sound of the blood pounding in her ears. So what if her cheeks were stinging and his dead-on gaze had her melting. So what if she'd gone momentarily mad. Any second now she'd be able to turn away from those big green eyes and that half-naked, supremely masculine body.

As he turned back to layer another blanket on the pallet, she didn't miss his amused expression. "And I missed you too," he said matter-of-factly.

If there was one thing she couldn't stand, it was the humiliation of someone laughing at her. "Tell it to your monkey," she said coldly as she headed for the ladder.

"Hold on," he said, starting up from his blankets. Lunging to catch her, he curved his arms around her waist and pulled her snugly against him. He took her elbow jabs with stoic silence, but that kick in the ankle warranted a four-letter response. "I got into that poker game to get information on Tony."

She didn't move, and for a long while she didn't speak. That was okay with him, because she was in his arms and not fighting to get away.

"It suits you to take me right to the edge, doesn't it?"

He made certain his lips brushed her ear when he whispered, "Allison, I haven't taken you to the edge . . . yet." He felt and heard her quick intake of air, and it sent his own desire higher. Angling his hips, he pressed his growing erection against the feminine curves of her backside. Moving against her, he made it tantilizingly obvious that she had him aroused. She held her breath until her body was resonating with tension.

"W-what did you find out about Tony?"

That she was now straining to keep her agenda in line sent a surge of masculine triumph through him. He cleared his throat as quietly as possible; at this point giving away his own emotional state was not something he wanted to do. "Tony's not coming through here for another week."

"Another week? What is he doing down here?" she demanded, trying without success to turn and look at him.

Reilly had his agenda too. Sliding his arm up her rib cage, he took on the supremely pleasant task of supporting the weight of her breasts, those just-big-enough breasts he wanted to make love to with his mouth and hands. "Tony will tell you all about that when you see him."

"And what about you?" she asked quietly. "Or am I not supposed to ask about you either?"

"You can ask."

"Just tell me *something*," she demanded in a desperate whisper.

"I'm here because you're here," he said,

snuggling in closer to wait for her surrender. Drawing his hand across her belly, he began rubbing it with with his fingers. "For seven more days and seven more nights." Outside the tree house thunder shook paradise, but inside Reilly waited for one small sigh. Her breathing deepened, and he knew it was only a matter of seconds before she was his. When she finally dropped her head back against his chest, he rocked her gently in his arms. "That's my girl."

"Who are you, Reilly?" she asked softly. "What are you doing running that awful hotel?"

Turning her around, he held her face between his palms. "I'm *here* because of you, and right now the rest of it doesn't matter."

Her gaze strayed to the pallet on the floor and then back to him. Placing her hands on his springy mat of chest hair, she shook her head. It was obvious that she didn't take these intimate matters lightly. When she spoke, her voice was warm and soft and doubtful.

"I don't know about this."

"Sure you do. You've known about this since the first day we met. And so have I."

Raising her brow was nothing more than a reflexive protest and, they both knew, a weak one at that. He responded to it anyway. "Baby, you can't leave now." Leaning his forehead against hers, he laughed softly. "Haven't you heard? It's a jungle out there." As he moved to unbutton her blouse, she stilled his hand with hers.

"Reilly?" She swallowed, then pulled at her lip with her teeth.

He waited for her question until he realized her eloquent look was all the question she could manage. He wanted to tell her that something more powerful than chemistry had preordained their next few hours. He wanted to spout a line of poetry to explain it or to call down bolts of blue lightning to circle around them. But he sensed that she wasn't asking for bells and whistles. Simply an answer from his heart.

"Allison," he whispered, "some things were meant to be."

The last of her doubt disappeared in a spreading grin that matched his own. She nodded slowly, teasing him with a pointed finger.

"You'd better be terrific."

"I'll do my best," he said, yanking off his boots and socks, then stripping away his damp slacks.

Peeling her blouse from her breasts and shoulders, she looked him over with tempting thoroughness. Her gaze lingered on his arousal.

"That's a good start."

Shrugging, he opened his palms to her. "I'm inspired," he said, watching her slide off her shorts, then nudge them aside with her toes. She circled him, devouring him unashamedly with her eyes as he did the same to her. Her proud carriage and sensual grace reminded him of a dancer . . . dancing privately for him. Before starting around him the second time she sent his clothes squarely on top of hers with a well-aimed kick. He nodded appreciatively. "Truly inspired." Without warning he reached for her with one hand and pulled her into his embrace. Contact with her body was like a slap of cool satin against his masculine length. "What about you?" he managed with a gasp.

Tracing his nipples with the pads of her thumbs, she looked up at him through lowered lashes.

"You can call me Al," she whispered before she kissed him.

He would have sworn he heard a sizzle as their lips touched, but the sound of her throaty moan was what thrilled him. Her glossy shell of civilized behavior had cracked wide open on that moan. Savoring the sound, he let her lead the kiss until he knew he had to respond from his own overflowing well of passion. He wanted to make love to her for hours, but somewhere between a look and a touch his plans began to change. Dipping his tongue inside, he explored the different textures of her mouth. "You taste so good. So damn good," he murmured. Twisting from side to side, she pressed her hips against his, caressing his burgeoning erection between the flat planes of their bellies. "Touch me with your body, Al. Touch me with all of it."

The daring command brought her hands off his chest and onto his buttocks. She lifted her knee, and he cupped the back of it, moving in closer to the center of paradise.

"We could be closer," she whispered.

"Much closer," he agreed, stirring the golden curls between them while he looked into her eyes. They were bright with desire and wide with expectation. Her parted lips strayed over his, but when he slid his finger inside her, she plunged her tongue deeply into his mouth. They stroked each other to a primal beat. Gently. Thoughtfully. Thoroughly. The air around them crackled as their storm of passion threatened to bring them down. When he eased in a second finger, she lifted her mouth from his and made the most exquisite sounds he'd ever heard. He felt her knee beginning to buckle, and he knew his wouldn't be far behind. Lifting his mouth from hers, he offered her his throat as he fought for more oxygen.

"We can do this standing. Or we can do it lying down. We just have to do it soon."

"Lying down." Lowering herself to her knees, she watched him join her, then smiled provocatively. "For now," she said while the tropical storm wrapped the bamboo tree house in billowy curtains of rain.

He nodded. "For now." Settling her back against the frayed red blanket, he stretched out beside her. Bracing himself on his forearm, he drank her in with hungry eyes. "There's a part of me that wants to stare at you forever . . . and then there's that part of me that doesn't."

"Close your eyes," she whispered, reaching up to take him in her arms. Moving into her embrace, he lowered his head between her breasts and began kissing her there. He took his time, placing each kiss on her skin like a fine jewel on satin.

She longed to feel him over her, to welcome his weight on her trembling body, but when she tried to urge him up, Reilly had a better idea.

Working his way along her body, he circled her navel with his wet tongue before continuing down. When his breath touched her thigh, a tremor of desire shook her. A few capable strokes, then a firecracker of pleasure was what she had expected, but he was taking her a whole new way to paradise—a long, secret way, exploring her with his lips and tongue. She hadn't anticipated *this* forbidden pleasure. This wild, intimate kiss she'd only heard about. In a series of gentle caresses, Reilly had her shifting restlessly beneath his attentions.

"Reilly, that feels . . . incredible."

Sinking her fingers through his hair, she wanted to hold him there. She also wanted more of him. All of him. "Come inside me," she whispered fervently as she fought the encroaching ecstasy with everything she had. But with a flick of his tongue the victory was his. Gripping his shoulders, she raised her hips in glorious surrender to the first wild wave of pleasure.

Lifting himself over her, he entered her on the second wave. Instinct had her wrapping her legs around him, and they held on to each other as if the world would burst apart if they let go. Crying out as one, they soared over the edge and all the way to the far side of paradise.

Even in the aftermath he wouldn't let go. Rolling to his side, he brought her with him, kissing her with untamed joy.

As she drifted down from the heights of ecstasy, she whispered, "Reilly, I never knew . . . I never knew."

He lifted his head. "Never, Al?"

"Never." The sweet moment lasted until she touched her fingertips to her blushing cheeks. Slipping from his embrace, she pushed up, resting her weight on her hip and hand. Walking her fingers playfully across his chest, she smiled to herself. "You were more than terrific."

Sometime during their throes of passion the tropical storm ended, and the jungle sounds began returning. With the mingling scents of cool rain and heated sex wafting around him, Reilly had never felt more in sync with paradise. In a moment of supreme male pride, he crossed his arms behind his head and leaned back to savor his woman. As rainwater dripped from the leaf tips in the surrounding branches, Allison looked on the scene with love-softened eyes. *Paradise*, he thought. A second later she reached for the touseled blanket, jerking it over her breasts.

"Damn you, Reilly. You promised me we

were alone," she said, pointing to the opposite side of the tree house.

Reilly curled to sit up, and twisted toward the ladder. There on the top rung sat Puddin' Head. Applauding.

SEVEN

The little monkey did a somersault, clapped again, then climbed over the bamboo rail and out onto a branch. Reilly roared with laughter, and soon Allison was laughing too. Wrapping the blanket around her, she followed Reilly to the rail to catch a glimpse of their audience of one.

"How did you ever find him?" she asked, peering through the leaves.

"He dragged himself up the steps of the Paradise Hotel the day after I took over. One of his legs was broken. He probably fell out of a tree. Anyway, I managed to knock him out with sweet wine. Then I set his leg."

"How did you know what to do?" she asked, watching Reilly take a fig from the basket on the table and toss it to the monkey.

"Premed school and the advice of the local healer from Chico's village."

"You were studying to be a doctor? How on earth did you go from premed to a poker game in Paradise?"

Leave it to sexual afterglow and Allison to make him run off at the mouth. Puffing his cheeks, he blew out quickly. If he didn't turn this conversation around, she would be insisting on the whole story.

In a friendly but impatient gesture, she tilted her head to one side. "Reilly?"

He hesitated.

She didn't. "Come on. After what we've been through, you can surely stop evading my questions. Who are you?"

"Let go of this, Al. Stop thinking about yesterdays and tomorrows," he said, stroking her shoulder. "Live in this moment with me. We'll make it last all week and maybe—"

"Reilly, I can't do that."

"Yes, you can. You already started over there on the blankets." He watched her eyes as she remembered. "Al, you were so deep in that moment with me."

Her gaze remained riveted to the pallet. "What happened over there was real."

"I know."

"What you're asking me to do is make a conscious decision to commit myself to a capricious notion. To live in a fantasy."

He watched panic playing leapfrog with possibility in her shifting expressions. "Yes, I am," he said quietly. As soon as he realized that his honest statement was beginning to unnerve her, he continued: "What's wrong with a little fantasy?"

"But I don't know anything about you."

"You know plenty," he said with a seductive grin. "And what you don't know doesn't count. Not now anyway and not here." Maneuvering behind her, he made certain she was facing into the canopy of the rain forest. "Look out at this emerald Eden where half those birds and most of those flowers don't even have names. Listen to the music of the monkeys and birds and . . . there, that sound. We'll probably never know what made it. Breathe it in, Al. Pull in a lungful of that sweet, musky perfume rising from the forest floor. It smells like us after we made love."

"It's all true," she said, her voice sounding far away, "but I don't know. I should go back to Pucalli. There's no good reason—"

"Don't be afraid of it," he said, turning her around, then running his hands down her arms. "Remember what you said that day in the river with me and Chico? 'No responsibilities. No worries. Just the pleasures of paradise and all the time in the world to enjoy them.' Come on, Al. You remember telling me that." He touched his chest. "Me." He looked her straight in the eye until she gave him a reluctant nod.

"Me," he said again, thumping his chest this time. "Me . . . Tarzan."

Slowly bringing a hand to her face, she covered everything but her eyes. She started backing toward the center of the tree house. He moved with her, step for step. Her pulse fluttered and her skin prickled all over as a series of thoughts claimed her mind. Reilly remembered her one whispery reference to her childhood hero. He had sensed the poignancy Tarzan's image held for her. Reilly was offering to bring the lord of the jungle to life in paradise. For her. If anyone could do it, Reilly could. And all she had to do was agree.

Enchanted by the mere suggestion, she allowed him to take her hand from her face. As he hit it against his chest, a roguish grin graced his face. "Tarzan," he said in a low, thundering voice that sent a ripple of laughter through her.

He thumped again, more emphatically this time. "Tarzan!"

She couldn't agree with him more.

Letting her blanket drop, she whispered, "My Tarzan." Moving closer, she traced his chin, then ran a hand over his hair and onto his shoulders. Tarzan's spirit. Tarzan's determination. Tarzan's flesh. "My very own Tarzan."

"Your very own," he said, scooping her up into his arms. She let out a tiny shriek of surprise, which quickly turned into a tempting giggle.

"Reilly, what are we doing?"

"It's what we're going to do," he said as he took her back to the railing and set her down. Leaning as if to kiss her, he drew his thumb across her lips, saying, "And I promise you, we're going to do everything. Starting right now."

"Everything?"

"At least twice," he said as he gently turned her around.

His fingers played along the indentation of her spine, before reaching around to cup her breasts. When he rimmed her ear with his tongue, her knees shimmied, then began to give. She would have gone down, but he braced her with his body against the half wall, whispering, "Not this time. Put your hands on the rail and don't let go."

She did as he asked, telling herself it was the only way to stop trembling. But the trembling increased as he kissed her down one thigh and up the other. Ribbons of pleasure were unfurling everywhere he touched her, everywhere he kissed her. Crisscrossing her back with his fingers, he nipped at her shoulder blades and the backs of her arms. His hot breath was stirring her to the core, enflaming her with desperate desire. When she started around to take him in her arms, he whispered again, "Don't let go."

Her fingers tightened around the thick bamboo. She gasped when he splayed his fingers over her hips and nudged himself against her with obvious intent.

"Reilly?"

He lowered his head to hers, nuzzling his nose against the side of her neck. "Hmmm?"

"Isn't this . . . the way the . . . monkeys do it?"

She felt the vibration of his laughter and the tickle of his chest hair against her shoulders. "If they don't, they will after tonight," he said.

"But I've never—"

"Shhh. Just relax and let nature take its

course." Tilting her hips forward, he eased himself inside her. "Everything okay?"

She shook her head.

"What's wrong?"

"You . . . stopped," she said, arching her body in blatant invitation for him to continue.

"Forgive me," he said, moving inside her with an urgency that surprised them both. "It won't happen again, I promise."

With firm flesh and relentless enthusiasm, he kept up his promise until, together, they shuddered into an erotic release that had the world quaking around them. Still inside her, he carefully reached forward, gripping the railing on either sides of her hands. The feel of his towering body, wrapped around hers, soon tamed her thundering heartbeat to a submissive purr. In the satisfying silence that followed she thought about the continuing intimacy of his embrace and the shameless way he was pulsing himself inside her. The pleasantly sensual stance soon flowered into need. Turning her head a fraction of an inch, she waited for him to say something. When she realized he was waiting for her, she pressed her smiling mouth against his jaw.

"I like a man who keeps his promises."

"At least twice," he said, setting himself to the task as she murmured encouragement.

Allison tipped up the brim of her pith helmet to look at *him*. Stripped to the waist and with his hair falling free, her lord of the jungle paddled their dugout with impressive skill. The cords in his wrists and arms twisted and pulled under glistening rivulets of sweat as he whipped the paddle port to starboard. She didn't try to hide the fact that she was openly staring at every masculine inch of him. She'd been doing it since they'd left Puddin' Head at the tree house two hours earlier.

Looking up from the river, he smiled at her. "Comfortable?" he asked, referring to the ferns he'd piled in the bow of the boat for her.

As she watched the tea-colored river purling around their dugout, she reached up to touch the liana vines growing down from branches above them. Exotic sounds mixed with the slap of Reilly's paddle as it broke the surface. "Perfectly comfortable," she said, resting her crossed ankles on the backpacks they'd brought for a few nights' stay deeper into the jungle. "Cleopatra's barge wasn't this well appointed."

"Careful," he said with a teasing wink. "You're mixing your fantasies, and this old body can't handle but one."

Squinting at him, she said, "I'd guess you are . . . thirty-two?"

"Just turned thirty-four."

She nodded as a dozen more questions flooded her mind. "Live in this moment with me," he'd said, and she fought to do just that. Most of the time he made it so easy for her. His spontaneity ruled their world, and she was a willing subject. He could be explaining the complexities of the Mayan calendar over their breakfast table and, with one arcing look, sweep the table clean and lay her back on it. Rolling her eyes at the memory, she pulled her pith helmet to the bridge of her nose and stifled a giggle. Wild man or gentle man, he was all hers for the rest of the week.

"Al," he said in a warning voice, "I can read your laughter like some people read minds, and getting it on in a dugout could leave us wetter than you think."

"Reilly Anderson! I am truly shocked that you think I—"

"Would think such bawdy thoughts," he said in a high-pitched attempt to imitate her voice as he stood up.

For one outrageous second she thought he was going to try making love in the dugout. Instead he took a bamboo pole from the bottom of the boat and lowered it into the water.

"Shallows," he explained, pushing them along. "The root system of that tree over there can reach all the way across this channel. If we snag, we'll have to wade to shore and portage."

That he would know this sort of thing didn't surprise her, but her natural curiosity about him kicked in again. From Mayan culture to fixing broken monkey bones, Reilly was a treasure trove of information. She'd even seen him catch a river fish, then reel off its nutritional value, right down to the calorie count. Maybe he had finished medical school. But then why wasn't he practicing medicine? More to the point, why was he wasting his time on the edge of civilization? She should have taken the opportunity to inspect the books lining the shelves in his room at the Paradise Hotel. Perhaps that would have filled in some of the empty spaces. Wrinkling her nose, she silently chastised herself. He wasn't applying for a mortgage loan; he was a rat-race dropout who, for reasons he kept to himself, was bent on enjoying an irresponsible lifestyle. She shifted uneasily on the ferns, knowing on some instinctual level that that wasn't his whole story. Even though he projected an air of general contentment, a more immediate mystery ruled him. Whatever that was was no concern of hers. And no matter what her heart was telling her, she wasn't falling in love with him. Love didn't happen in a few weeks. Did it? She sat up slowly, holding on to the freeboard and staring hard at Reilly.

Easing back into her fern nest, she told herself that just because he whispered the most incredible things in her ear when they made love didn't mean he loved her. All of it was part of the fantasy he was creating for her. While it lasted, she could *pretend* she was in love with him. She pressed her hands to her chest; she was too responsible a woman to lose her heart in carnal reverie.

"What's that look for?" he asked.

"Nothing," she said, feeling her heart beat a little faster under her fingers. Sliding one hand down the other, she began fiddling with the safety chain on her watch as she studied him. First the muscular columns that were his legs and then the way his hips and waist flared out into a rock-hard chest and strong, wide shoulders. Sunlight was striping him like a moving tiger as he flexed his knees and twisted his upper body to keep his balance. The power of his physicality was mesmerizing. "You're beautiful, Reilly." *So beautiful, I swear, I could take a bite out of you.*

"Tarzan handsome," he said in a gutteral voice. "Allison beautiful."

A toucan squawked from an overhanging branch.

"Bird agree with Tarzan," he said, jerking his head in a convincing parody of the fictional character.

She did not love him, she loved the way he made her feel. Yes, that was it. Only right now he made her feel like . . . crying. How utterly ridiculous, she told herself as she tried to control the warm tears blurring her vision. Pretending she was wiping perspiration from her face, she swallowed hard and forced an air of the curious tourist into her voice.

"Reilly, speaking of beautiful, have you ever seen the resplendent quetzal? I hear it's considered by many to be the most beautiful bird in the Americas."

"I haven't seen it yet. It lives in the cloud forest. The vegetation is so lush up there that it's hard to spot it with its emerald-colored feathers."

"The vegetation is lusher than this?" she

asked, waving her hands toward the living green tunnel they were drifting through.

"It's like a greenhouse gone mad up there. The plants pull their moisture from mist-laden air. Orchids, bromeliads, ferns, mosses all growing on top of each other." He shook his head with awe. "The Paradise cloud forest is the most amazing place I've ever seen."

Sliding the pole to the floor of the dugout, Reilly sat down and resumed paddling. She was about to ask him more about the cloud forest when she caught sight of movement along the shore.

"Reilly?" she whispered, leaning forward. "I thought I saw someone over there."

"Very good, Miss Richards. They've been trailing us for the last half hour."

"They? Who are *they* and what are they doing out in the middle of nowhere?"

"They are members of one of the last tribes living in this rain forest. And this might look like the middle of nowhere to you," he said, directing the dugout toward the right-hand side of the river, "but if you lived in Callamarto, you'd be home right now."

Allison jerked her head around to see a dozen half-naked people walking toward the river. The sound of their laughter filled the air.

As the dugout glided into shore, several barely clothed children splashed in after the canoe. Reilly slipped over the side, and with the help of the children quickly pulled the craft ashore. Before she had a chance to ask questions, four women walked into ankle-deep water, crowded around Allison, and began stroking her hair. Reilly spoke to them, half in what Allison recognized as Spanish and half in another language.

"They're talking about my hair, aren't they?"

"Yes."

"Well, what are they saying?" she asked as one of the women removed her combs. Allison's blond hair tumbled to her shoulder, making the women gasp and jump back.

"Nothing important. They want to know if I'd trade it for a bucket of the local brew."

"My hair?" she asked, snatching a lock out of one woman's hand. "I hope you told them no."

"I said I'd consider it for a cold six-pack of Budweiser," he said, heading up the incline.

"Reilly! Wait. Don't leave me here," she shouted, jumping out of the dugout and almost upsetting it.

He came back for her and, taking her hand,

began leading her up the riverbank. "Come on. I won't let anyone cut it."

"But what about our backpacks? Shouldn't we bring them with us?"

"Allison, look around you. These people don't know how to steal. The rain forest gives them everything they need," he explained quietly as one of the women placed Allison's haircombs back into her hand.

"But what about—?"

"Mortgage payments? Videos?" He looked at a woman nursing her baby. "Infant formula? God help them, that's all yet in their future."

The slight edge to his voice took Allison by surprise. This was the first time he'd sounded genuinely upset in days. So, she thought as she breathed in the smoky air from the village's cooking fire, Reilly was tipping his hand again and in the process causing her curiosity to return. "I just meant, what if . . . they get sick?"

"That's the least of their sorrows. You're standing in the middle of one of the biggest natural pharmacies on the planet. Unless El Diablo Timber Company gets possession and runs it through a sawmill."

"Oh, they wouldn't!" she said, whipping around to Reilly. "Would they?"

He stared at her for half a minute before throwing his arm over her shoulder. "Tarzan won't let that happen, Al," he said, walking her toward one of several stilt houses. When he realized her smile hadn't returned, he casually added, "Anyway, that stuff happens only in Brazil."

"Oh," she said, sighing loudly.

"Wait here," he said, starting up a step ramp. "I've got business with the chief."

"The chief? You bring me all the way out here, and I don't get to meet the chief?"

Waving her toward him, he gave her a fake frown. "I don't suppose you'll ever let me hear the end of it if I don't introduce you."

She scampered up after him. "What business with the chief?"

"Permission to travel through his land."

"Am I supposed to bow or something?" she asked, ducking through the doorway after him.

"Your best bet is to sit in the corner and shut up," he said, pulling her into the smoke-scented interior.

"Well, you don't have to be rude about this," she said, shoving her hands to her hips and glaring at him.

"Rude is not the issue. Chief Atotico would probably like a blonde as his third wife and—"

"Say no more." Backing into a corner, she sat down and waited until her eyes began adjusting to the dark. Then she saw the chief. Except for an upper-arm ornament, the chief looked no different than the others she'd seen in the village. Bright, brown almond-shaped eyes, shiny black hair, and even-toned brown skin. Pulling her knees to her chest, she drank in every detail of the scene. The thatched roof, the roughly hewn floor, the fiber hammocks, and the strange pipe the chief was smoking. Safely tucked away in the corner, she began spinning an adventure including Reilly, the tribe, and Chief Atotico. While Reilly spoke to the chief in respectful tones in the center of the stilt house, Allison soon lost herself in a jungle-rescue daydream, including poison blow darts, fire walking, and Reilly in a loincloth. Just as he swung down on a vine to scoop her away from death, Reilly called her name.

"What did you say?" she asked, startled back into reality.

"He wants to see your watch."

"My watch? My parents gave me this for my—"

"You'll get it back."

She slipped the watch from her wrist and held it out to Reilly.

"He wants you to hand it to him."

This was like a scene out of a movie, she thought, as she crossed the room to where the chief was sitting. A quieter sort of movie than she had been playing in her mind. One with comedic undertones, she added, when she heard the chief laughing like a child. Bowing, she squatted down on her haunches to hand the watch to him. "Does he want me to show him how the alarm works?"

"That won't be necessary," Reilly said. "I think he just wanted to see you close up."

"I understand his curiosity. I wanted to see him close up too," she said, studying the tatooed markings curling along his forehead and cheekbones.

The chief spoke to Reilly.

"What's he saying now?" she asked.

"He wants to know if he can touch your hair."

Smiling at the chief, she lifted a lock toward him. "Is it the color that fascinates them?"

"That and the way it curls."

The chief spoke again, and Reilly translated. "He wants to know if you'd like to touch a part of him."

Reilly's gaze connected with hers, and what started out as a hesitant moment of consideration rapidly turned into something else. The innocent exchange suddenly became charged with a lighthearted sexuality among the three of them. Shaking her head, she stood up, saying, "No, thank you."

Reilly guided her back toward the step ramp.

"Good answer," he said to her. "Colors and sizes may vary, but as far as I know, they only come in two styles and you'd be better off guessing at the chief's."

"I believe you're right," she said, managing a good-bye wave and a muted giggle before Reilly pulled her out the door.

They left Callamarto on foot, following their guides, two volunteer villagers, higher up into the rain forest. Allison's legs were aching by the second hour of their journey, but Reilly's high level of energy inspired her to continue. When they stopped at the end of the third hour, Reilly had the men place the supplies they'd been carrying on the ground. After a verbal exchange the two villagers bowed respectfully to both of them, then started back down the trail.

"They're leaving us here?" Allison asked, her voice hinting at possible panic.

"For a couple of days. They'll return when it's time," Reilly said, helping her off with her backpack. "Let me see your scarf." When she handed it over, he stood behind her and blindfolded her.

"Is this where I get to break open the piñata? she asked.

"No," he said, lifting her up in his arms and carrying her forward.

"Okay," she said thoughtfully. "Are you making sure I won't be able to find my way here again? You know, like when someone's taken to a secret rendezvous point."

"Nothing so melodramatic, my little daydreamer. I wanted you to get the full impact of this place, all at once." A minute later he put her on her feet and whisked away the blindfold.

Her mouth dropped open, but she remained speechless for several seconds. "Oh my God, Reilly. This looks like the place in the candy-bar commercial," she whispered finally. Clutching at his arms, she shook them as she tried to speak. After several tries she gave up and sat down by the thatched hut at the edge of the perfectly circular pool he'd brought her to. All around them dozens of brilliant blue butterflies were fluttering through the air. Through a curtain of flowering liana vines dangling from branches overhanging the pool, she could see and hear two waterfalls. She looked up at Reilly, who'd taken off his shoes. He knelt down and removed one of hers.

"Happy birthday, Al," he said, taking off the second.

"But . . . it's not my birthday."

"Oh," he said, as his deadpan expression turned into a frown. "Guess we'd better go, then." Getting to his feet, he turned to leave.

"Not on your life," she said, pulling him back for a kiss.

As the kiss continued, he pulled her to her feet, then picked her up again and started toward the pool. When he lifted his mouth from hers, she rested her head on his shoulder and sighed.

"I always envisioned *this* part of the fantasy with them naked."

He stopped, then started backing out of the pool. "I love it when you speak your mind," he said, setting her on her feet.

They were out of their clothes and back in the clear, blue-green water in less than a minute. She leaned back, letting her hair float around her in honey-colored streamers. Nearby a bird called sweetly to its mate while Reilly's hair tickled her behind as he swam under her. He popped out of the water, shoving his hair back from his face. Even as she smiled at him, her eyes were drifting closed.

"What is this place?"

"Callamarto's honeymoon hotel. Only newly married couples can use it to consummate their marriage."

"How did we get in?"

"Guess," he said, massaging her feet.

"You lied to the chief?" Spreading out her arms, she busied herself by using them to keep her body perfectly aligned. Meeting his gaze while they were talking about marriage brought her closer to a reality she was trying not to think about. She thought about it anyway. *She was not falling in love with him*.

"I stretched the truth," he said, rubbing her toes against his chin as he watched her face. "You look all dreamy-eyed, Al. I guess that uphill hike tuckered you out."

"I'm relaxing, that's all," she said insistently, as the ache in her muscles began dissolving to a pleasant heat. "How could anyone close her eyes and miss even a moment of this?" Rolling her glance around the edges of the pool, she ended up smiling drowsily at Reilly. "Not me, not one heavenly moment."

Standing up in the chest-high water, he

moved closer and cradled her upper body in his arms. "We have plenty of time," he said, his image looming over her. Bending down to kiss her forehead, he whispered, "All the time in the world."

The combination of his warm caress and the cool, watery weightlessness lulled her to the edge of slumber. She whispered his name, wanting him in her semiconscious state to answer a question she didn't have the energy to ask. A question that melted into other unasked questions. Crazy questions about mortgage loans and character references and where to build a house. She whispered his name again. Or maybe she thought she'd whispered his name. She wasn't sure . . . about anything, only that she was slipping into an all-encompassing sense of uncertainty.

"Shhh. I've got you, Al. I won't let you go."

EIGHT

"You want me to do what?" she asked, looking at the giant tree on the other side of the pool.

"Swim over with me and climb that tree." He pointed to a sturdy limb projecting out over the water. "I put a surprise up there for you while you were sleeping this afternoon."

"The ladder back at the tree house is fine, but climbing up through the branches . . . I don't know," she said, wrinkling her nose in embarrassed apology. "I'm not very good at climbing."

"With legs like yours, you must have been a tree climber when you were a kid?"

Rubbing the fingers of one hand, she looked at her legs. "Not really." Breaking into the fantasy with sad facts was the last thing she wanted to do. Well, next to the last, she corrected as she looked at the huge tree across the water.

"Then, darling," he said, taking her hand and walking her toward the water. "Isn't it about time you learned?"

"I could live without this experience," she said, dragging her feet on the shore.

"But I couldn't live without seeing your face when you find my surprise," he said.

Ten minutes later, after she'd changed into her two-piece, chamois-colored bathing suit and they had swum across the pool, he was carefully guiding her out on the primary limb with him.

"Trust yourself. You're not going to fall. This isn't a branch on your backyard cherry tree, Al. It's as broad as a sofa cushion. That's it, just put your hand here and step over the clump of leaves."

When she'd joined him on the other side, he let her catch her breath before he lifted his chin toward a crotch in the tree.

"Your surprise."

"It's a knotted rope," she said after staring at it for five seconds.

His eager, closed-mouth nod prompted her to speak with more enthusiasm than she felt.

"Wow. What is it attached to?" she asked,

not daring to lean closer in case she would topple thirty feet to the water.

"Al," he said, comically pretending to lose his patience, "the rope is attached to the tree. See?" He pointed upward and outward from where they were standing.

"I can see that part," she said, winding her fingers more tightly around the branch by her hips. "What am I supposed to do with it?"

"It's what we're supposed to do with it. Think Tarzan and lianas, or in this case a strong rope, and you'll have today's activity figured out. Got it yet?" He waited until she turned her face toward his. "How in hell do you get your eyes to open that wide?"

"You mean for us to swing through this tree out over the water?"

He smiled broadly. "And then let go."

"Oh, I don't think so," she said, checking back to see how she was going to climb down to the ground. "But I'll watch you." Lifting her foot to step over the leaf clump, she continued nervously, "It was a great idea, Reilly. I used to love watching Tarzan do this in the movies, but—" She saw and felt Reilly's hand close around her wrist. Her gaze traveled up his arm to his face. "What?"

"We'll ride it out together."

For a few seconds guilt replaced her fear. After taking the trouble to plan this surprise, he had had to lug the rope in his pack, then fix it to the tree while she was sleeping. What he didn't know and could not have known, was that when it came to derring-do, she had less experience than a china doll. She studied a spray of baby orchids growing between them. "Reilly, you don't understand—"

"You're afraid."

"Petrified. I'm telling you the truth when I say I never did this stuff as a child. I'm sorry, but you'd better forget you planned this for me." She did a double take. "Now what are you smiling for?"

"Maybe Reilly could forget, but you're not dealing with Reilly. You're dealing with Tarzan." Picking up the rope, he let the bottom ten feet of it drop before positioning his hands over his carefully selected knots. Pressing his back against a branch, he gave her a once-over look. "Jane would have done it for Tarzan," he said before wrapping his feet above a large knot and leaping.

Watching Reilly swing through the branches and over the pool was the crowning moment in the realization of her childhood fantasy, but when he let loose with Tarzan's clarion call, all hell broke loose inside her. He was riding the rope like a perfectly weighted pendulum, his slow-motion sortie heading straight into her little-girl heart. By the time he'd let go, she was asking herself, *Why not me?* and as he hit the water, she was bracing herself to catch the rope on its return.

Allison was in a crouch position, rope in hand, by the time he'd surfaced. She could see him straining for a look at her, but the thick foliage prevented him from seeing her.

"You want me to come up and help you climb down?" he asked, swimming to shore. He stood up, knee-deep in blue-green water.

"Stay where you are," she shouted back as she wrapped herself around the rope. Fear was returning, but she told herself she could channel that into her own clarion call. Then she took the plunge, only hers wasn't a streamlined flight like his. Dropping straight through the branches, she barely swung clear of the tree as she heard her call progress straight to a scream. She hung on for her life.

"Let go. Al, let go. Oh, sh—!!"

She hit him squarely in the chest, knocking them both down on the ground and sending them rolling out of the water and into the mud. When they finally stopped, he was on top of her, partly straddling her. Pushing up on his knees, he looked down into a disoriented pair of blue eyes.

"You were supposed to let go."

"I was trying to be spontaneous," she whispered before her eyes slowly closed.

"Al?" Shoving back the hair falling in his face, he shook her gently. "Al, don't joke with me," he said, carefully crawling off her. When she didn't open her eyes, he splashed water on her face. "Wake up, wake up," he whispered. Her lids fluttered as she tried to say his name. She was out again.

There was next to nothing he could do with her on this side of the pool. Since the first-aid kit was in the hut, he quickly made a decision to take her back there. Lifting her into his arms, he looked to either side for the easiest path around the pool. Swearing through his teeth, he realized his problem. The upper and lower waterfalls prevented him from carrying her on land. In the end he walked back into the water and began swimming across, with Allison in the classic rescue hold. "You're going to be okay," he said, more to himself than to her. After lifting her out of the water, Reilly gently placed her on the mossy ground, then tore into his backpack until he'd located the first-aid kit and the smelling salts. Before he had it under her nose, he was cracking open the cloth-covered ammonia capsule. They both jerked back from the fumes.

"Take it easy," he was saying as she fought her way out of the bottom of a black hole. She landed a solid blow on his flesh before her vision cleared. "Hey, you hit hard for a girl."

When she was finally able to focus, she looked up at Reilly. His concerned expression was as far from carefree as she could have imagined. As she tried lifting herself up on her elbows, he held her down with one hand while he fished in his pack with the other.

"Try not to move. How's your head?" he asked, pulling a small flashlight from the side pocket.

She rubbed a place on the side of her forehead. "Awwwww. It hurts," she said, looking up at him with embarrassment. "I was so stupid. I thought I could do it, Reilly." Her voice trailed off in a whisper. "I thought I could be spontaneous like you and . . . let go and have fun."

"You weren't supposed to have that much fun," he said, lifting her eyelids and checking her pupils.

"How many fingers am I holding up?"

"One . . . Dr. Anderson."

"I'm not a doctor."

"But you've had medical training," she said before blinking the light from her eyes and connecting with his gaze.

He looked away, busying himself with stuffing the minilight into the side pocket. Pulling herself to a sitting position, she touched her palm to his bare chest as she continued looking at him. "We thought we could forget who we are, didn't we? Me for a week, you for I don't know how long."

"The past isn't important, Al. It's who we are now." Looking around them, he attempted to dismiss her serious tone. "No more head bopping. Okay?"

She sighed long and hard. "I deserved that head bopping."

"You what?" he asked.

"Reilly, I let myself forget . . . some things."

He handed her a fruit drink from one of the supply packs. "Let's get this confession over with so that we can get back to what we were doing. What things?" he asked, humoring her concern.

"Things like when Susan and I were children, she almost died."

Dropping his chin in disbelief, he asked, "From falling out of a tree?"

"No, from an illness. She's fine now, but when she was so sick, she used to tell me she wanted to be like me. That's quite an ego trip for an eight-year-old. As her illness wore on, I came to feel more and more responsible for her. I remember thinking, *What would Susan do without me?*" Allison drew her knees up and wrapped her arms around them. "She needed my help then, and she needs it now."

"Al, you make it sound like you kept her alive. You were just a little girl too—"

"But I did keep her alive. I gave her my bone marrow."

He stared at her without blinking. "Leukemia."

She smiled softly. "Yes."

"God, Al. I had no idea."

"I'm sure Tony thinks we spoiled Susan, but we didn't think she'd make it to her fifth birthday." Allison looked across the pool at the rope dangling several feet above the surface. "The doctors assure us that she's healthy and that the baby is healthy, but it's not easy believing it after what we went through with her."

"You've had your hands full, haven't you?"

"And I can't say I've regretted giving up

part of my childhood for her. You see, I consider myself blessed because I still have her. Reilly, she's the most enchanting, loving creature you could imagine meeting. And she is so in love with Tony. Whatever their problem is—"

"Your sister hasn't given you a clue?"

Allison shook her head. "No, and on top of that we can't figure out why he hasn't been answering her letters. After she received that one from him with the Paradise Hotel as the return address, she must have sent him over a dozen. Why would he put her through hell by not writing back?"

"Al, there haven't been more than three letters delivered to the Paradise Hotel for Tony, and they all arrived quite recently. In fact, just days before you did. He simply didn't receive them. Truth is the mail delivery in this country isn't worth the price of a stamp."

"This is all so crazy. Why would he give up a perfectly good job and come out here beyond the edge of civilization?" When Reilly didn't offer any explanation, she attempted to control the growing frustration she heard in her own voice. It was no use. She was still bewildered. "I just don't understand. He's a good—"

"Don't upset yourself, Al. I'm sure this

mystery will all come together when you finally meet with Tony."

"But you can't imagine what it's like watching Susan, pregnant with their baby, wondering where her husband is. How he is. Or even if he's still alive." A wave of anxiety knocked into her. She grabbed Reilly with both hands. "Oh, Lord, Reilly, he's not dead, is he?"

"No, no, no," he whispered reassuringly, taking her into his arms. "He's alive and well," he said, feeling her tension as she leaned against his chest.

"I believe you."

He knew by her shaky voice that she still held doubts, and he couldn't blame her. As beautiful as Paradise was, she understood the isolation and, therefore, the inherent danger. Allison's anguish was tearing at his resolve. Telling her he knew where Tony was and what he was doing there would only prompt more questions. Questions about his own connection to the project, about why he hadn't told her, about the potential danger from El Diablo Timber Company, and so many more questions he'd lost count. And for now answers to those questions were to be avoided at all costs. On the other hand she was reaching out to him in a way that was getting to him.

He had to give her something to hold on to.

He had to give her a part of himself.

Moving her from his chest, he looked into her eyes. "Al, I *can* imagine what it's like watching Susan go through this."

"You can?"

"Yes, I can because my mother went through it for over twelve years."

She sat up then, brushing her hair out of her face. "Tell me."

"My father was declared missing in action during Vietnam. Eventually my mother gave up on ever seeing my father alive again. She remarried. Probably out of loneliness and to help raise her children. Whatever the reason, that second marriage failed. That's when I quit medical school to help her out. Hell, Al, you would never give up on something or someone you believed in. You can't imagine how much I admire you for that."

The moment shimmered around them, so filled with emotion, there wasn't room for words. Finally Reilly spoke. "Let's go back to where we were before you flattened me to the ground." Fixing a hopeful smile on his face, he cocked his chin and waited.

"Let me say this, Reilly."

"And then we'll not be serious?" he said, hoping to extract a binding promise.

She nodded. "I'm sorry about your father, but now that you told me, I know you're telling me the truth about Tony. You'd take me to him if you could, because if anyone understands my need to find him quickly, you do, Reilly. And that's because you're more than a good guy. You're a decent man," she said, curling into his arms. "And to think I doubted you. I must have been crazy."

She trusted him. It took him several seconds to close his arms around her. Several empty seconds that were followed by a full plate of guilt. She trusted him. Now. But wait until he told her what he'd known all along. Pulling her close, he touched his lips to the slight swelling on her forehead and felt her wince. "Sorry, I didn't mean to hurt you."

"Of course you didn't mean to hurt me," she whispered.

"I wouldn't intentionally."

"I know that." She pulled away, looking at him with a radiant smile on her face. "This is wonderful. I feel so much better now that I told you about Susan and me. And that you understand because of what's happened in your own life. But you look so serious. I thought we weren't going to be serious."

He stared at her long and hard. He was wavering again. If he told her now that he'd known all along where Tony was, the rest of their time together most likely would be a disaster. With the few remaining days left on the project, it would also be a waste of time trekking up into the cloud forest for Tony. Tony would be back at the Paradise Hotel to greet them when they returned. Smoothing back her hair, he decided to wait until the last possible moment to explain how he had come to remain silent about Tony. In the meantime he would offer her subtle hints of his own responsibilities while he prayed like a mad zealot for her eventual understanding. Even a decent man could suffer poor judgment on occasion. And was there anything wrong with wanting to give her back her childhood, plus those other pleasures that had nothing to do with childhood?

"Reilly? Were you going to say something?" she asked.

Holding her face in his hands, he kissed the tip of her nose. "Only that it's great to have my playmate back." *And that I love you*. From the lingering intensity in her blue eyes, he wondered if he'd spoken. What was he waiting for anyway? Why not say those words and see what happened? He laughed quietly, and she joined him. Yes. Why not set the rest of their lives into motion? She loved him too. Maybe she hadn't said the words, but he felt it.

Touching her bruise, she hesitated. "My head hurts," she said, bringing her other hand to her head. Her steadiness began wavering. "I'm a little dizzy—" Her voice trailed as her body pitched forward into his arms.

"Al, darling, you have to stop flinging yourself into my arms like this. It's way too romantic." His lighthearted words belied Reilly's thundering heart. If her injury turned out to be serious, he'd never forgive himself. Her eyes fluttered open, and a weak smile lifted one side of her mouth."

"No more smelling salts. I'm not passing out. I'm just closing my eyes."

"The butterflies will be as happy to hear that as I am. When I snapped open that ammonia capsule before, a cloud of blue morphos took off. One more whiff of that stuff and they'll think I'm out to pin them."

Her giggle was stopped short by a wince. "If I rest for a few minutes, I'm sure I'll be fine by tonight," she said, slowly lifting her head.

"You're going to rest for more than a few minutes. I've got your whole night planned."

She gave him a pained-looking smile. "You have no idea how I hate saying this, but I do have to say it: Not tonight, dear, I have a splitting headache."

"I wasn't talking about making love to you, I was talking about checking your pupils in case you've had a mild concussion. I'm not letting you sleep more than fifteen minutes at a stretch."

"But—"

"Not a word of protest," he said, settling her comfortably before he put together a light meal for them.

Reilly kept her occupied by telling her stories about running the Paradise Hotel. He was careful not to mention Tony Church and was surprised that she didn't mention him either. The first time she slept, he draped the area in mosquito netting and fixed a small light overhead. The light reflected off the gauzy netting, surrounding her sleeping form with an iridescent glow. Unfortunately the ethereal scene was causing him more concern than enjoyment. Bringing to mind the fantasy they'd both agreed to resume, he was wondering once again what she was going to say once the fantasy ended. Once she heard the truth about his connection with Tony, would she be so eager to think of him as a decent man? Would she understand that he'd decided to keep silent to ensure that he had as much carefree time with her as possible? He pictured her, terribly upset with him that he hadn't told her immediately. Or at least when she'd revealed that private and painful time in her young life.

Tucking an improvised pillow under her head, he sat back in the indigo shadows to watch her.

When he'd first met her, he had envisioned her in her tempting pastel lingerie. The vision no longer fascinated him. At least not when she was wearing this two-piece chamois-colored bathing suit with the raw-edged hems that looked as if they'd been stylishly ripped by Tarzan himself.

Laughing softly, Reilly remembered their first meeting and being impressed that she looked as if she had been sculpted from a breath mint. Knowing her intimately now, he had to admit he liked the warm feel and dewy scent of her just fine. She'd given up makeup, allowing her skin to develop a honey-colored tan, and pulled her hair back in an untamed mass that held more appeal than any intricate hairdo.

Besides, there was no lipstick to smear or coiffure to mess when they made love. What more could he ask from life than this? Allison, lying on a bed of emerald moss in all her natural splendor. Standing, he moved closer for a better look. This should have been enough to hold him in the moment, but he couldn't deny the reality of things to come. Their *moment* would end in unknown reckoning. Sinking to his haunches, he plowed his fingers through his hair, then dropped his elbows onto his knees. Their future looked uncertain, but not impossible. If he kept his mouth shut, they'd have this time together to make their relationship even stronger. Strong enough for her to understand and accept.

"But I want to try the rope again," she insisted later the next morning while she helped him bundle up the mosquito netting.

"No."

"I promise I'll let go of it this time. I know I can do it."

"I'm sure you think you can, but my heart couldn't stand the shock of seeing you knocked out again," he said, stashing the netting inside the door of the hut.

While he was bending over, a creamy-white petal, the size of her hand, floated down to Reilly's back. Picking it up, Allison drew it along his arm, then circled his lower back with it. "Well, I feel ready for something," she insisted.

"Really?"

"Really," she said, confirming it with a pinch to his butt.

Turning around, he sat down on the camp stool and held out his hands to her. When she took one, he pulled her astride his thighs, and settled her weight there. "What's got into you?" he asked before inhaling the sweet fragrance of the petal she held.

Dragging the petal over his eyelids and around his ears, Allison leaned in closer and began nibbling at the underside of his chin. "You got into me," she murmured, squirming seductively on his lap. Pulling her mouth away from his, she watched his reaction through lowered lashes. He dropped his head back and hooted. "Well, you did," she said, stuffing the petal into his mouth, then thumping him as he sputtered it out and continued with his laughing. "You probably *planned* for this to happen, didn't you?" she asked, watching a second and then a third petal float to the ground beside them.

"Planned for what to happen?" he asked, stroking the outside of her thighs until he had his hands around her bottom.

"To see me turn into a wanton, begging you for one thrill after another." Sliding her hands over the tops of his shoulders, she squeezed him gently as she pushed her bottom lip into a pout.

"Don't do that with your mouth," he said, groaning theatrically and grabbing the sides of the stool.

"Would you prefer me doing something else with it?" she asked, batting away a falling petal. Breaking their connected gazes, they stopped their sexual teasing long enough to look upward and watch more petals floating through the air.

"What's happening?" Raising her hands, palms up, she began catching them. "Are there monkeys up there shaking the branches?"

"No," he said, bringing himself under control. "You're in for a rare treat. The tops of the tallest trees can burst into bloom at unpredictable intervals and within twenty-four hours drop every one of their petals."

Standing, she backed off his lap and looked

up into the canopy. "Oh, Reilly, this is like being in a glass ball. You know. The kind you shake and snow falls on the scene inside."

The symbolism didn't escape him. That glass ball she was talking about protected a perfectly staged moment where time had no meaning. A carefully chosen fantasy moment where the drama ended peacefully, happily everytime. The one glorious difference from their situation was that *he was in this moment* with Allison, drifting along in a bubble of sensual delight.

He leaned back against the hut to watch her in the petal shower. She reminded him of a first-time beachcomber collecting every clamshell on the beach. The crook of one arm was soon filled with petals, but she kept on catching more. He couldn't have asked for anything prettier, except that bruise on her head to disappear. Smiling, he welcomed the pleasant sensations of growing desire within him.

"Look, they're falling into the pool and sliding over the lower waterfall."

"Postcard pretty, for sure. But you ought to come and sit down. We have to keep an eye on that bump."

She'd been with him long enough to recognize that fakely innocent sound in his voice.

Since the bruise was old business, Reilly wasn't interested in it, and neither was she. With an outrageously burlesque like sway to her hips, she moved slowly back to where he sat. "You've been keeping an eye on my 'bumps' since the moment you met me." Licking her lips, she leaned forward as if she was going to kiss him, but stuck out her tongue and dumped the petals over his head instead.

"Damn right I have," he said, brushing them off his face, then reaching up for her. "Let's have a look."

"You'll have to catch me first," she said, starting around the pool toward the upper waterfall.

The camp stool went tumbling as he shot to his feet to follow her through the falling petals.

Her high-spirited laughter mixed with the sound of the falling water. She stopped once. Turning her head and shoulders in his direction, she made certain he was close behind before she slipped behind the thin curtain of water. The cooled, moisture-laden space darkened when he reached the entrance. Ducking under a rocky outcrop, he stepped inside and slipped his arms around her.

"Gotcha!"

Stroking his shoulders, she drew him

closer. "No, Reilly, I've got you," she said, practically shouting above the din of the waterfall. Reaching down, she molded her fingers to him.

Covering her hand with one of his, he spoke loud enough for her to hear. "That . . . bump on your head. Maybe we shouldn't—"

"I think we should."

Pressing the edges of her teeth to one of his nipples, she tugged gently. By the tremors playing against her lips, she knew his heart was beating faster. So was hers, bringing pulsing heat to every place he would touch her. Kiss her. Tease her. Trailing kisses over his chest, she absorbed the sensation of his unabashed growl. "You're mine. Every magnificient inch of you," she said against his crisp mat of chest hair. "And I'm never going to let you go . . . because I love you."

She looked up, but he didn't reply. For a few seconds she wondered if she'd taken their game too far. Maybe he didn't want to hear any reference to time beyond this moment.

"You can say anything you want to," he shouted, moving his hands to stroke the material covering her breasts. Her nipples strained against the thin chamois, until he lifted the material from her body. "And I won't hear a thing you're saying." He leaned closer to her ear. "So make it naughty."

She made it naughty. So naughty her ears were burning and her breath was coming in tight little gasps. And by his firm and burgeoning response, he was getting the message. When he reached for her, she pushed him back against the rock and began working her way down his front. Her fingers arrived at his waistband before her mouth. Easing down the elastic with agonizing slowness, she continued telling him what she was going to do with him. Telling him what he was going to do to her. She felt his trembling fingers sliding through her hair, half caressing her and half intent on not hurrying her. Taking him in her hand, she guided him toward her now silent mouth. Looking up, she caught his smoldering gaze in hers. He was trying to tell her something, but in the watery shadows it was impossible to read his lips.

Dragging her up the front of him, he spoke loudly enough for her to hear this time. "Do this in the sunlight. For me." He kissed her quickly when he saw her brows knit together in question. "Because I want to see you."

She didn't hesitate. Taking his hand, she led him from the shadows and out onto the petal-strewn ground. They made it as far as the first patch of sunlight, when he stopped her.

"Here?"

He nodded. Slipping out of his shorts, he continued watching her, waiting for her next move.

The air was ripe with the pungent perfume of fallen flowers, tangy sweet and hypnotic. She watched his chest rise as he pulled in a lungful of air. Powerful shafts of sunlight struck his gold-tipped mane of hair, creating a nimbus around his head and shoulders. Her gaze slid over the rest of his body as she removed the bottom half of her suit. All of him in sunlight was too godlike to touch, but too inviting not to. She swallowed hard, feverishly aware of her desire for him. Her pulse was pounding like a jungle drum, sending a shameless mating call that she was about to answer. She looked up at his face again. His golden-green eyes darkened, and she knew he was listening to the same call in his pulse. Their world shrank to a seductive touch, a brazen stroke, and looks that felt like one long, tender caress.

"Reilly," she whispered, stepping forward to rub her face against the solid wall of muscle that was his chest. "I . . ." she began, before lavishing attention on his nipples with her lips and tongue.

"Tell me," he whispered as she slid down the front of him to her knees.

She stroked his arms, kissed his hands, then pulled his hip against her cheek. "Reilly, I want you so bad, I'd kill someone if I had to end this now."

Fitting her mouth over his hard male heat, she began the intimate kiss with a delicate swirl of her tongue. He tasted wild. Hot. Right. Tightening her lips around him, she gripped the backs of his thighs and slipped into a primal rhythm as old as love.

Reilly watched her, reveling in the full force of her fantasy. He felt the pull in his heart, his head, his soul. Every sweet move she made was a loving gift to him. But it couldn't go on. Not much longer anyway. The need to spill himself inside her was rushing forward like a storm-swollen river.

"Baby, wait," he whispered as his splayed fingers slid across her face. She released him, kissing the hard plane of his belly and the corded, bulging muscles in his thighs. Her lovestorm of kisses continued, bringing him down to his knees. "You're right," he managed to say in a rough whisper. "Why wait?"

Breathy laughter escaped her lips as she tumbled him sideways to the ground. Reilly took her with him, pressing her back into the petals, then quickly covering her body with his. Poised above her, he hesitated then pressed his lips to hers, opening them in a painfully soft kiss.

Achy heat spread from her tingling lips to the liquid heat between her thighs. Moving feverishly beneath him only served to sweeten his kiss. His control was admirable, but under these circumstances, close to driving her mad. Rocking against him, she pushed up on his hips until she could claim his firm flesh again. He moved to accommodate her, urging her with a primitive growl to make the most of her capture before guiding him to his rightful place.

As he entered her, the petal-smooth center of her body closed around him in a profusion of snug contractions. Glorying in her feminine rite of possession, he rolled to his other side, taking her with him. Petals crushed beneath them as her throaty sounds joined with his, calling out to the life around them. *This was their place in paradise.*

Afterward Reilly lay on his stomach beside her, watching her watching him. Holding her hand in his, he kissed her fingers, then pressed them to his face. With creamy-white petals tangled in her hair, her lips still ripe and red from his kisses, and her eyes dewy with emotion, she reminded him of a fallen angel. She curled her body toward him, resting her cheek in the crook of her elbow. Now was the right time to tell her about his connection to Tony and Taylor Pharmaceutical. He'd make a clean breast of it, and in this glorious afterglow she would understand that he had meant the best with his decision to keep quiet. Pulling a petal from her hair, he was about to speak when she looked up at him.

"Reilly?"

"Hmmm?"

"I know I already apologized for this, but I must have been crazy to think you were any more involved with Tony than taking his mail." She stroked his back, trailing her fingertips along his spine. "I know when I look in those big green eyes of yours that you're incapable of holding back the truth. You would have taken me to Tony if you knew where he was. Will you forgive me for not trusting you sooner? For doubting you?"

"Aw, Al," he said, sitting up and rubbing his brow. His newfound courage was crumbling. How could he confess to her now, when she'd just told him he could walk on water? "Let's not talk about this."

"But I want to get this out in the open. I feel guilty about ever doubting your integrity."

"Shhh," he said, pulling her into his arms so that he wouldn't have to look into those earnest blue eyes of hers a split second longer than necessary. He'd never felt such apprehension about losing a woman, but Allison had him paralyzed with fear.

NINE

"How do we thank them, Reilly?" Allison asked as they walked into the village of Callamarto a few days later. "What can we do to show them how grateful we are to them for letting us stay at the falls?"

"Teaching our guides the short version of 'that strange and wonderful song from your village' will be a lasting statement of our gratitude," he said dryly as they watched their two guides teaching "Louie Louie" to their friends.

When Reilly cocked an eyebrow, Allison knew he was teasing. "Seriously, Reilly. We can't walk away from here without letting them know how privileged we feel." She reached to pick up a little girl clinging to her leg. The child began playing with Allison's hair, sinking her fingers into the one braid resting on her shoulder.

"We'll ask for a visit with the chief. Showing him respect for their hospitality is all they ask and all they really expect." He reached to tickle the little girl in Allison's arms. "Besides, what do we have that they could possibly want?"

As Reilly started toward the chief's house, Allison touched his arm. "Wait. What about you, Reilly? How am I ever going to thank you?"

He looked at a fixed point on the ground. "No need to thank me."

When he started away again, she held him back. "But everything that happened up there," she said warmly, motioning with her head toward the trail, "mattered a lot to me. I feel like a new person." Holding him, she stroked his arm with her thumb to underscore the point. "I don't know if you can understand, but—"

"I understand," he said, cutting her off while his gaze settled on her wrist. After a second his gaze drifted to the ground again.

What began as a friendly gesture was turning into an emotion-packed exchange. Allison looked at the child on her hip while she tried to swallow back the tears. Her voice was whispery and shaky. "No, you don't. For once in my life I got to be outrageous and free and irresponsible. I got to be a little girl again, and I had the neatest playmate anyone could ever dream of having." Setting the child on the ground, she unwound the tiny fingers from her hair, then turned her attention to Reilly again. "And for the rest of the time I had the most wonderful lover any woman could ever want." She pressed her hand to her chest, as she struggled to get the words out. "You took care of me."

For one moment she thought he was going to take her in his arms. He took a quick breath and looked toward a nearby stilt house. Maybe he hadn't said he loved her, but she knew he did. She knew because he told her with his touch, his laughter, and the way he whispered her name. She knew it best of all when he was beyond whispering.

He was shaking his head. "Let's go get your watch back."

His jolt of humility was endearing. Or maybe what she was seeing wasn't humility. She smiled at him as the next logical thought presented itself. Once she would have screamed at his evasiveness, but she was beginning to understand. He still hadn't shared the secrets of his own life. He had been too busy listening while she was pouring her heart out to him. Or maybe he put off telling her because he wasn't sure she could handle his secrets. Especially the dark ones, like what awful thing had brought him to this place. She wanted to tell him that she was ready to hear the worst, that she believed he was a decent man, and that, if he asked her, she could make a drastic change in her life for him. Staring at his strong profile, his sleek ponytail, and his beautifully muscled body, she realized that her words would be the second-best way to convince him. Reilly was a man of action. What he needed was dramatic and tangible evidence that she was now the kind of woman who could adapt her lifestyle to his. Giving his arm a reassuring squeeze, she waved him off. "Go on. Thank Chief Atotico for me. I'll be all right here. I have something I want to do."

Ten minutes later Allison waited at the bottom of the step ramp outside the chief's house. A few dozen villagers were forming a half circle around her, murmuring their surprise as they moved closer. She calmly accepted the small-sized spectacle she was creating. Carefully turning her gift over in her hands, she finally held it aloft so that the rest of the villagers could view it.

Reilly emerged from the house with the chief at his side. He stopped short when he saw what she had done, but the chief continued toward her.

"Translate for me, Reilly," she said, placing her cut-off braid into the chief's hands. She nodded respectfully to the chief, then locked her gaze to Reilly's. "Tell the chief that these past days have filled up the empty spaces in my life and the empty places in my heart. Tell him I learned to leap and let go. And tell him I loved every minute of it."

As Reilly rushed to translate, Allison turned and walked toward the river and their dugout. If he didn't know before, *Reilly knows now*, she thought triumphantly. *He knows the message was meant for him. He knows I love him.* And because he knew, she could wait; the next move was Reilly's.

When he joined her there, he quietly went to work lashing their few remaining supplies to the center of the canoe. Strangely at peace with her dramatic gesture, Allison watched Reilly's solemn expression. He was deep in his own thoughts, working his way through her stunning action and what it meant for them. She was sure of it.

"Aren't you going to say something . . . about my hair?"

"How many cups of that instant coffee did you have this morning?" Reilly finally asked as he tested the strength of his knots.

He was trying to make light of her message, but she wasn't having it. Not one bit, she thought warmly. "Cutting off my hair had nothing to do with my caffeine intake. I was being spontaneous not rash, when I decided to leave a part of myself there."

He nodded. "Not rash? Well, I guess this means I can store my machete next to you and not have to worry about losing anything if I happen to nod off."

"Your ponytail's safe with me."

"Who said I was talking about my ponytail?"

She pressed her lips together, trying not to laugh. When she gave into the urge, he smiled too. "Are you always going to treat moments like this with humor?"

"It's part of my charm." He tapped the center seat with his fingers. "Scoot over here."

Allison carefully maneuvered herself to the center, then took hold of either side of the dugout. After he rolled into the canoe, several villagers pushed them out into the river. As he paddled to the middle of the waterway, she twisted around to wave one last time before they disappeared around the bend. When she turned back, she caught him looking at her hair.

"Reilly," she said softly, as she ran her fingers through her hair. "I don't regret this. There was something wonderfully liberating about the act. It was sort of like leaping from the tree on the rope. Well, when you finally let me leap. I thought I'd never talk you into that." Off in the distance she could hear the strains of "Louie Louie." Reilly kept on looking at her hair. "I guess you think it's unattractive."

"Not at all."

"I will be getting it professionally shaped, and I haven't seen it in a mirror yet, but still . . . it feels right." Dipping her hands into the water, she slicked back the sides, moistening the mass into a fresh and different look. "I feel right."

Reilly kept on a steady, even paddling as they stared into each other's eyes. He ducked once to avoid the tail feathers of a low-flying bird. After a while he spoke. "Speaking of cutting things short, Al, we stayed an extra day at the falls."

Allison lowered her hands to her mouth. "Oh. I stopped counting the days."

"I didn't, but there's no reason to get upset. You'll get to see Tony in a very few days."

"Okay."

"Okay?"

She shrugged. "I trust you. You wouldn't lie to me."

Reilly suddenly didn't seem to know where to look.

"I left word with one of the poker players in Pucalli that Tony should go on to the Paradise Hotel if he didn't connect with me by yesterday. We'll pick up Chico and head back downriver as soon as possible."

She chose her next words with care, making them purposely cryptic and, hopefully, vaguely comforting. "I'm not worried. I'm sure everything is going to work out." Unfortunately Reilly didn't look the least bit comforted.

They picked up Chico the next day and caught the first boat out of Pucalli. While Allison praised their good connections, Reilly's mood sank lower. Watching Chico and Allison at the rail of the riverboat, he was reminded that time was skipping merrily forward. And nothing was working out as he'd planned. He'd even brought Puddin' Head back with them. The monkey tugged on Reilly's ear, chattering happily when Reilly handed him another piece of fruit. The little bugger couldn't wait to get back to the dinner table at the Paradise Hotel now that Allison was hand-feeding him too. Reilly sighed wearily. He could see his future; he would end up with a pocket-sized monkey and without the woman he had fallen in love with. He looked up as Allison waved to him. She and Chico were engaged in an animated discussion that Reilly knew they would bring to him in, he guessed, the next two and half minutes.

"Reilly!" Chico shouted. "You gotta listen to this," Chico said, as he ran toward him with Allison following. "Tell him, lady. Tell him how we can bring *mi padre* home."

"It's just an idea, mind you," she began as she maneuvered around a cage filled with parakeets. "First you hire Chico's father to help you lengthen the dock in front of the hotel. Once that's done, this riverboat can start letting off and picking up passengers."

"Yeah, Reilly. You gotta make it *más largo*.

Then lotsa people could spend their money. Go on, lady. Tell him."

"In the meantime you can start improvements on the hotel. Chico tells me his father is the handyman around the logging camp. He'll be able to help with just about anything. Put in a few more bathrooms, maybe add a few rooms off the back. Your business is bound to increase, and you'll always have need of a full-time employee."

Standing behind Chico, she slid her hands over the boy's shoulders and hugged him to her. Chico accepted the affectionate hold with a chipped-tooth grin and a contented sigh.

Stroking the monkey's tail, Reilly leaned back in the deck chair. "I thought you couldn't stand the Paradise Hotel."

"She couldin' stand *you*, Reilly, but she changed. She like you a lot now. She think you a good guy. Right, lady?" he asked, looking up at her.

"Right," she said, casting a quick glance toward Reilly. "I think you're a good guy, Reilly. And as for the Paradise Hotel . . . well, I didn't think I'd ever admit this, but the place does have a certain charm." Stretching out in the deck chair, she sighed and closed her eyes. "Think about the idea."

Think about it, the lady said. Right now he had all he could do to keep his brain from exploding. Volunteering for another eight months in San Rafael for Taylor Pharmaceuticals was the last thing he could picture himself doing. Then again, remodeling the hotel would be an excellent cover for him. And sooner or later the company would be sending more employees if the project expanded. A company-owned hotel would eliminate a housing problem. In the meantime, if Allison continued being so understanding, Paradise would be a hell of a fun place to start married life. What did he have to lose? Besides, any plan that would strengthen their bond might come in handy when she discovered he'd been holding out on her.

Reilly squinted into the sunlight, studying the boy hopping along a nearby row of empty deck chairs. "Ever since El Diablo began beating the bushes for workers, families all over San Rafael have suffered," he said quietly to Allison. "Everywhere you go, you see sad-faced children. I think the only thing sadder are the faces of the wives. It isn't right that families are separated for months at a time, even if the money is good." He shook his head at the sad state of affairs. "Can you imagine what it's like for Chico and his brothers and sisters? Or for his mother, missing her husband?" The words were out before he could think to stop them. He didn't bother trying to hide his wince.

Allison turned her head toward Reilly, but kept her eyes closed against the bright sunlight. "I sure can. My sister has been going through the same thing for months."

Those lips, that tongue! One minute they were working miracles and the next they were massacring what was left of him. He rubbed his brow, then motioned the boy toward him. "Chico."

The boy did a hopscotching series of jumps across the deck and onto their deck chairs. "Yeah?"

"When does your father's contract run out with El Diablo?"

"*Mi padre* don't got no contract 'cause he don't cut the trees."

"You think he would quit El Diablo to come work for me?"

"Sí." Chico scrambled down beside him and moved closer to the armrest, closing his hands around Reilly's wrist. "You gonna do it? You gonna bring him back home?"

Allison opened one eye.

Reilly swallowed.

"I have to check on a few things first, but I think so." Reilly expected another explosion of energy from the child. Another whoop. A few somersaults. A loud announcement to every passenger and crewman on board. What he didn't expect were the tears welling up in those big brown eyes. The boy dropped his head against Reilly's chest and sobbed.

"*Gracias*, Reilly. You a good guy."

Allison sat up and dropped her feet to the deck. Patting Chico's back, she looked at Reilly. "You realize this is turning into quite a habit for you, don't you?"

"What's that?"

"Fulfilling a child's dream."

He'd have to cut down on the time he spent staring into her eyes. He still had to keep a clear head if he wanted to get through their meeting this evening with Tony. Leaning across the boy, he kissed her softly for several seconds.

"Oh, Reilly," she said, sighing, then patted his cheek. "I can't tell you how much I admire your integrity."

Reilly wore his smile like a piece of dead wood. Guilt weighed him back against his chair. No matter what happened, his life would never be normal again. His peaceful days in paradise were over. As sure as God made green bananas, Taylor Pharmaceuticals would have to airlift him out of there in a straitjacket.

"I see him! Reilly, I see Tony. There on the dock," Allison shouted over the roar of the float-plane engine. In her excitement she beat on Reilly's thighs. "Look! He's grown a beard."

Reilly wanted to think he couldn't feel any lower than he did right now. Unfortunately he knew that probably wasn't true. He pressed back into the seat to allow Allison an unobstructed view of her brother-in-law. She leaned closer to the window, waving madly.

"He doesn't know it's me, Reilly. Oh, is he ever in for a surprise."

Reilly nodded like a wise man. "I think we're all in for a surprise."

Several minutes later Tony Church clapped his hands to the top of his head as Reilly lifted Allison onto the dock. "Allison? What are you doing here? Is something wrong with Susan?"

"Susan is fine," she said, giving him a hug.

Tony reached around her to offer Reilly his hand and a puzzled expression. "What are you doing here, Allison? What's going on? What happened to your hair?"

"Allison came down here about a . . . family matter, Tony."

"Family matter." Tony shoved his hands through his hair and sat down wearily on a piling. "I knew it. Susan wants a divorce."

Kneeling at his feet, Allison sat back on her heels and smiled up at her brother-in-law. "Tony, she wants the father of her unborn baby home where he belongs."

Tony raised his head, looking from Allison to Reilly and back to Allison. "Baby? She's going to have a baby? I'm going to be a daddy?"

Chico crossed his arms and shook his head. "*Mi padre* always looks like that when *mi madre* tells him she gonna have a baby. I'm goin' home." Running up the dock, he turned back once. "*Gracias.*"

Grabbing Allison's hands, Tony squeezed them. "Susan's okay, right? She's really . . . healthy?"

"She's glowing."

"I'm going to be a daddy," Tony said to Reilly, as if he were announcing the news for the first time. His dazed expression continued as he turned toward Allison. "When am I going to be a daddy?"

Allison clasped her hands under her chin and smiled. "Less than five months."

The news set off a burst of manic energy in the father-to-be. Standing up, he pulled Allison with him and started dancing her around the pile of luggage and cargo. "Less than five months! Have I been gone so long?"

"You sure have," said Allison. "What have you been doing down here?" She didn't miss the look exchanged between the two men. "Well?"

"I've been doing field research for a pharmaceutical company. It's very hush-hush at this stage of the project. My part wraps up in another week. Two at the most, and then I'm on my way home to Susan." He looked at Reilly. "There are several good reasons to celebrate. Let's open a few beers, buddy."

A smile lifted a corner of Reilly's mouth as he nodded weakly. "I could use a cold one right about now."

"Sounds good, pal." Tony looked from Reilly to Allison and back again. His eyes narrowed with curiosity. "Where have you two been?"

Reilly was getting that sinking feeling again. This little laugh fest couldn't go on much longer.

"Reilly and I have been having the most marvelous time, Tony." She closed the space between her and Reilly, slipping an arm through his as she spoke. "We've been everywhere. In a tree house in the jungle, canoeing on a river without a name, marching up and down a mountain with the heaviest pack you can imagine." She bumped Reilly with her hip. "I never thought I'd get that kink out of my back."

"That kink out of your back? Ha! That's a laugh," Reilly said, teasing her with a tilt of his chin. Her blue eyes were twinkling up at his as she recounted their adventure. Maybe he was too pessimistic with his assessment. Maybe she would understand or at least forgive him, because if that wasn't love shining in her eyes, he deserved a double bout of malaria. "After you fell out of that tree, I had to carry you back to the hut."

"Big deal." Pulling away from him, she shoved her hands on her hips and turned toward her brother-in-law. "He forgot to tell you that I was under water most of the way."

Reilly leaned toward Tony, jabbing his index finger in the air. "She's right. Otherwise I'd be in traction."

Allison gave in to a fit of laughter, collapsing onto Reilly's outstretched arm.

"How long have you been in San Rafael?" Tony asked, eyeing their intimate exchange with a knowing look.

She shrugged. "A week or two. Who keeps track of time down here? I mean, once we made it out of Pucalli and into the jungle—"

"Pucalli? Reilly, why didn't you bring her up to me?"

Her lighthearted expression changed to cautious confusion. "What?" She took a step toward Tony. "You kept moving around, and we kept missing you. Reilly didn't know where you were."

"The hell he didn't. I was glued to my microscope up at the station. Reilly's the one who took me to it in the first place. He hasn't been up there in three weeks." Smiling at Allison, he continued. "And I think I can see why. You've been busy."

She looked blankly at Reilly for several seconds. "You knew?"

Reilly stroked his ponytail. "We're going to have to talk about this, Al."

"Look, I don't know what's going on between you two," said Tony, "but it's obvious to me that you have something to straighten out. Why don't I leave you alone for a bit?" No one bothered to answer him. Tony quietly began backing away toward land. "Right. So I'll see you two later."

Reilly reached to slide his arm around her shoulders. "Al."

"Don't touch me," she said, stepping back and raising both hands. "Don't you come near me."

"I know I probably allowed this to go on for too long, but—"

Ignoring his diplomatic tone, Allison started in on him. "You knew exactly where Tony was all this time? You could have taken me to him? Get away! You knew what finding him quickly meant to me. You could have explained all this to me . . . a million times?" Stepping over their luggage, she bumped into the pilot as he climbed back into the plane.

"Al, sweetheart, something pretty special started happening, and I didn't—"

"Something special? I don't know what you're talking about. That was all a childish fantasy."

"Childish fantasy? Are you crazy?"

"Not anymore," she said, picking her backpack out of the pile.

"We can talk this out, Al." As the plane engine roared to life, Reilly's voice roared too. "We're good at talking."

"No, we're not. You're good at lying," she shouted, stepping onto the pontoon. Pounding on the door, she shouted to the pilot. "Wait! Get me out of here."

"What the hell . . . ?" Reilly grabbed her arm, but she shoved him back. "Are you forgetting everything that happened between us up there?" he asked, pointing upriver.

"Nothing happened up there, you reprehensible, lying, irresponsible, no-good—" The tears stinging her eyes never made it to her cheeks. The prop wash blew them away as quickly as they appeared. The plane's roar grew louder, making it impossible for her to hear her own voice. Holding her hair away from her forehead, she yelled, "I can't believe I cut it. I must have been nuts!" She stopped shouting long enough to realize her throat was hurting, not to mention her head and heart. There was nothing more to say anyway. Turning away from him, she yanked the door open, climbed inside, and slammed it shut.

"Where to, lady?"

"As far away from Reilly Anderson as you can take me."

The pilot looked out her window. "Reilly's still talking to you. You sure you want to—"

"Fly this damn thing, mister," she said, slapping away her tears, "or I swear I'll fly it for you."

"Yes, ma'am."

TEN

"I should never have mentioned Reilly Anderson to you. You have enough to worry about without listening to my mess," Allison said, sinking deeper into her sister's cushy armchair and wrapping an arm around her knees. Allison looked over the wad of tissues she held to her nose. "I should be taking care of you." Blowing her nose, she wiped it roughly while motioning with her other hand. "I've always taken care of you."

Susan Church calmly poured another cup of herbal tea, squeezed in honey from the plastic bear dispenser, and handed the cup to her sister. "When is someone, anyone, in this family going to realize that I'm capable of a little nurturing? I haven't been actively dying for at least fourteen years. In fact I'm so full of life, I throw up," she said, rubbing her rounded tummy. "That reminds me. While you were doing the wild thing with your lord of the jungle, did you happen to think about birth control?"

Allison stared at her sister's protruding midsection and felt that odd ache of disappointment again. Setting her cup of tea aside, she dropped her feet to the floor, sat up, and sighed. "I got my period last week."

"You don't sound relieved."

"What?" Allison felt her startled expression quickly turn to a frown. "Of course, I'm relieved. I mean, I've never acted so irresponsibly on so many levels in all my life. My bank president says he's never allowing me vacation time again, and I think he means it. What was I thinking of?"

"Obviously not Costa Rica. So you tell me, Allie."

Allison sliced through the air with her arm. "No. I don't want to talk anymore about Reilly Anderson, except to say that he lies very well."

"There's got to be more to his story than what he's told you. I can't believe my well-balanced, thoroughly logical, and intensely perceptive sister would fall for a poker-playing, ne'er-do-well dropout just because he fills out a loincloth like a Chippendale hunk."

"I said I *thought* he would look good in a loincloth. Did I tell you he does birdcalls too?" Allison flopped back into her chair and covered her eyes with her hands. "I can't believe I said that. What's happening to me? I can't even hide in my hair anymore," she said, pulling on the short strands.

"You're in love, Allie."

"I can't be," she protested weakly. "I shouldn't be. I'd have to be crazy to. What was I thinking of?" her voice trailed off.

"What *were* you thinking of?"

Standing up, Allison walked a few steps to the door of the nursery while she tried to figure out the answer. "I don't know. Maybe I was thinking about those smiley-face sunflowers we painted on the walls in there. And about how happy you and Tony used to be. Or maybe I wasn't thinking at all." Raising her arms, she crossed her hands over her collarbone. "I told Reilly . . . so many things. Straight from my heart, Susan. I could have sworn he understood how important your situation is. He was very convincing. He really, really was. That's why his not telling me that he knew where Tony was makes no sense."

Nothing concerning Reilly made sense except that she had to stop talking about him. And thinking about him. And missing him. Shoving her fingers through her hair, she turned away from the nursery and forced a smile on her face. "Anyway, Tony's coming back, and that's what I went down there for. He sounded awfully happy and eager about seeing you and delighted about the baby. He probably feels terrible about leaving you."

Susan folded her hands over her swollen middle. "Tony didn't leave me. I asked him to go."

Allison blinked. "You know, for a second there, I thought you said you asked Tony to go." The room remained strangely silent. "Susan?" When her sister kept on staring at the chair across from her, Allison sat down in it. "I went all the way to San Rafael to find Tony for you and—"

"I never asked you to go."

"But—"

"And no one in our family asked what happened between Tony and me. They assumed Tony flipped out and poor little Susan was left with nothing." Raising her eyebrows, Susan looked down at her oversized blouse and smiled a knowing smile.

"Don't stop now," said Allison, waving her wad of tissues for her sister to continue.

"Well, thanks to your bone marrow, I got over my leukemia. The problem I continue to face is that no one else got over it. No one, including Tony, listens when I tell them I am a healthy, capable person who can handle my own life." She reached for Allison's hands, squeezing them. "I was suffocating with so much attention. I had to do something drastic to make Tony understand. I just didn't think he'd leave the country."

Allison nodded slowly. "I see."

"Please don't take this wrong, but I'm not your dying sister anymore, I'm okay now. And I think Tony and I can work things out. I just wish he'd get back here."

"He'll be back," Allison said softly. She was looking at Susan as if she were a stranger. After a while she sat back in her chair. "You really are a grown-up, aren't you?"

"I'd better be," she said, taking Allison's hand and placing it on her belly. "Feel that."

The baby gave a hearty kick, and Allison looked up in astonishment. "That's amazing."

"I can't wait to share this with Tony."

The door swung open behind them. "Tony

can't wait either," he said, walking into the room. "Hello, darling."

Susan was on her feet and in Tony's arms in an instant. Between kisses the two of them were saying all the things Allison had imagined they might. The scene wrenched at Allison's heart, making her envious and sad and happy all at the same time. As much of an uncivilized bastard as Reilly had turned out to be, she was reminded how much she continued to miss him. Longing for a moment like Tony and Susan's, Allison knew she had to get out of there or scream.

"You're beautiful," Tony told his wife. "Isn't she beautiful, Allison?"

"Beautiful," she agree, heading for the door. "I'll leave you two alone." When she tried to pass them, Tony's hand shot out, stopping her.

"Hold on a minute. I have a message for you."

"If it's from Reilly, I don't think I want to hear."

He grabbed her wrist. "Then listen to what I have to say."

"Don't, Tony. You need to be alone with your wife."

Tony looked down at Susan. "I intend to be very soon. In fact, when you leave I'm locking the door for a month. So let me get this out now."

"It's over, Tony. I need to put that time behind me."

"I was doing contract work for Taylor Pharmaceuticals."

Bewildered by Tony's insistence to talk about his time in San Rafael, Allison looked at Susan, then back at Tony. "Susan said you made regular deposits into her checking account. Whatever our family thought of you, we knew you didn't leave her to starve."

"That's not what I'm getting at. Reilly Anderson works for Taylor Pharmaceuticals too."

She rolled her eyes in disbelief. "I can't imagine why they gave him a job. He wasn't exactly knocking himself out keeping that hotel running."

"The Paradise Hotel is Reilly's cover." Tony sent a loaded look over his wife's head to his sister-in-law.

"What are you talking about?" Susan asked when words failed Allison.

"About a year ago a team of German botanists pulled out of the region when one of their men . . . disappeared. El Diablo Timber doesn't want that northern rain forest up by

Pucalli set aside for research. While I was hunting up bromeliad specimens to convince the San Rafael government to do that, Reilly was coordinating the project and keeping us alive." Letting go of Allison's wrist, Tony gave his wife a reassuring hug. "I trusted Reilly with my life. He's a good guy, Allison."

A good guy. Wasn't that what she'd once called him? And a decent one too? Allison ruffled her hair at the back of her neck, then threw up her hands. "Why didn't he tell me all this?" she asked, suddenly angry and confused.

"I can't answer that," Tony said, looking into Susan's adoring gaze. He brushed his lips against his wife's. "But I'd get going fast if I were in your shoes."

"I'm sorry," Allison said, trying to figure out exactly who and what she was angry at. "I'm going back to my place to sort this out. You two ought to be alone."

"I meant, I wouldn't wait around here much longer because Reilly's assignment is about to end. When I asked him if I'd see him up here anytime soon, he said he wasn't planning a trip back here for quite a while."

"Well, where's he going?" she asked, her pulse pounding in her head.

Tony shrugged. "Anywhere he wants to go.

Taylor Pharmaceuticals' golden boy of marketing is due for some mega time off. So if you want a chance to talk this out with him—"

"Susan—" Allison interrupted as she lowered herself into a starting-block stance and grabbed her purse from the sofa table.

"I'll call your office," she said, leaning over her husband's arm to receive a glancing kiss from her sister. "Good luck."

"Welcome home, Tony," Allison said before hurrying out the door and pulling it closed behind her.

Allison had gone over several possible dialogues on the flight down. She had even gone so far as to furnish Reilly's responses. The closer she came to the Paradise Hotel, the more nervous she became. "A lover's spat," she murmured walking up the stairs to the wooden walkway. No. That wouldn't do, she decided as she wiped perspiration from her forehead. Sounded too much like a news flash. "So what if I called you all those names? You didn't really think I meant them." She stopped and shook her head. Too glib. Absolutely not. "A combination of PMS and that bonk on the head. I'm right as rain now, Reilly," she whispered to herself, after she noticed the thunderhead approaching. There. That sounded good. Just the right amount of humor and pathos.

Confidence began returning until she spotted Reilly from the wooden walkway. Allison's first impulse was to race up the steps of the Paradise Hotel and head straight to his hammock. Then a niggling fear started in her stomach. She swallowed and began a steady walk up the stairs and across the veranda, pausing a few feet away.

Casually sprawled in the hammock, his fully clothed body made a powerful statement of invitation. "DéJà vu, all over again," she said before nervous laughter bubbled up. He stirred and started to move his hands from behind his head. "No, don't get up yet. And keep that hat over your face because I can't quite look you in the eye yet. That's a new hat, isn't it? Australian, I think." Lacing her fingers together, she squeezed them hard. Was she going to babble all day?! As if in answer, a huge clap of thunder prompted her to speak. "Look, you've got to know I didn't mean all those horrible names I called you." She took a step closer and kneeled beside the hammock. Dragging her fingers along the edge of it, she studied his belt. That was new too. "I mean, after those days and nights in the tree house with you, and all that time at the pool . . . well, I still dream about us. Especially that time by the waterfall. You were every fantasy come true, Tarzan," she whispered, lifting the brim of his hat. "My Tarzan. My very own—" She let out a scream and jumped to her feet. "You're not Reilly!" she shouted to the dark-haired man smiling up at her from the hammock.

"I'm not Tarzan either."

Shock turned into embarrassment as she stared into a handsome face and a pair of pale-blue eyes. Once, she might have felt a beginning twinge of interest in his amused expression and those extraordinary blue eyes, but Reilly Anderson had branded himself to every fiber of her being. "Where is he? Where's Reilly Anderson?" When the man in the hammock didn't answer, a panicky feeling snaked through her. "I didn't miss him, did I?"

"I'm right here."

Whirling around, she saw him in the open window of the bar not four feet behind her. He stood with his shoulder against the window frame, his arms crossed over his open, sage-green shirt, and his eyes riveted to hers. He'd tricked her again, and even though she wanted those gorgeous arms around her, she also wanted to stay mad at him. That wasn't going to be easy, but she'd do her best. He looked even better than her memory of him, and that was saying a lot. She swallowed, as her gaze slid to the khaki shorts barely covering his navel. "How long have you been standing there?"

"Long enough to want you to say all those things again," he said, climbing barefoot over the windowsill. "Only this time say them to me."

She glared at him, fighting to keep up her shield of anger. No matter that the late-afternoon light was bathing him in sepia and gold and adding an air of rich indolence to his cocky grin, she had a right to be ticked. "You let me say all those things, those *personal* things to, to—" She motioned with both hands toward the hammock. "Who is this guy?"

"Jack Stratford," came a voice from the hammock. "Reilly, does she come with the place?"

"No, she does not," Allison and Reilly replied in unison.

"I should have known," he said, replacing his hat over his face.

Allison wanted to believe she could continue staring at Reilly for as long as it took to wipe the candy-eating grin from his face. But she would never know how long that was. At that moment the Bartolino sisters, Reverend Phillips, and Mr. Garfield appeared from around one corner of the veranda. Chico came racing from the other side with two hammers in his hands.

They all started talking at once.

"We thought we heard your voice, dear."

"When you screamed, I told *mi padre*, 'The lady's back. Maybe she bring my tip.'"

Allison nodded. "I did."

"Praise the Lord, you've returned to the fold."

"Awright, pretty momma."

Allison waved her fingers at all of them before raising both hands against Reilly's bare chest. His face kept on coming toward hers, blinding her with its smile. "Hold on," she said, fighting the sizzling sensations streaming over her once she'd touched him. "Don't you have some explaining to do?"

"I have some kissing to do. Can't I explain later?" he said, easing his hips closer to hers, then sliding his fingers into her hair.

She jerked back from his smooth and seamless advance. "Later?"

The Bartolino sisters began giggling.

Chico dropped his hammers and covered his ears.

Reverend Phillips murmured something about a blessed moment.

Mr. Garfield began humming "Love Me Tender."

And Jack Stratford lifted the brim of his hat, then dropped it back into place.

Allison looked into Reilly's face, and the six others present ceased to exist. Pushing out of his embrace, she shook her finger at Reilly. "No, you cannot explain this later. You're already a month late with it. Why didn't you tell me you knew where Tony was once we got to the tree house? Once we—" She started walking backward along the veranda. "Don't look at me that way."

Reilly opened his hands and looked at the group and then to Allison. "What way?" he asked, pretending an air of shocked innocence.

"And don't you dare give up without a fight. I'm not ready to forgive you yet."

"I'm ready to forgive you," he said, following in her footsteps. The rest of the group, minus Jack Stratford, followed at Reilly's heels like a ten-legged puppy.

Jamming her fists to her hips, Allison stopped and stood her ground. This was not the romantic reunion she had hoped for. Reilly was being much too lighthearted about her complaint, while her eyes were stinging with the first hint of tears. "You disappoint me, Reilly."

"That's a first," he whispered, leering comically in her direction as his gaze roamed brazenly over her. His relief at seeing her and hearing her had gone straight from his heart to his ego. While she definitely had a point that he had some explaining to do, he had the answer to his prayers—he had his woman back, and he wanted the world to know. Or at least the residents of the Paradise Hotel. Continuing to tease her was nothing more than a celebration of his happiness. When his gaze returned to her shimmering blue eyes, he knew he'd gone too far with it.

"All right, be that way, Reilly. But you're not walking away from this without hearing me. While you were tricking me into believing you were sympathetic to my sister's situation," she said, slamming her hand to her chest, "I was falling in love with you! So there."

"Before flames start shooting out your ears, I have something to say. While *we* were living out *your* Tarzan fantasy, I was falling in love with you. Only that was no childish fantasy, Al."

The group began to cheer.

"Well, if you loved me so much, why didn't you tell me the truth? What did you think I'd do?" She moved closer, thumping him soundly on his chest. "Tell the whole world your secrets?" Slapping away a betraying tear, she struggled to stop her chin from trembling.

"Come on," he said soberly, reaching for her hand. She allowed him to pull her the few extra steps to his room. The ten-legged puppy was right behind them. "Time out," he announced to the group before taking Allison inside and gently closing the door on them.

Allison folded her arms and made her way to the other side of his room.

Except for the group's diminishing chatter, nothing but Allison's cool and wary look existed. For the first time since she returned, he felt a quiver of anxiety in his gut. She might have said she loved him, but she hadn't said it lovingly. Not yet. And who could blame her when she wasn't sure she could trust him?

"Make it good, Reilly."

Her simply-put request had him weak at the knees. Laced through her words was the unspoken message that she had her pride and that she also had about all she could take. He sank wearily onto his bed and leaned his elbows on his knees.

"When you showed up here looking for Tony, my company had less than a month left before our project ended. If Tony found out about the baby before completing his research, I wasn't sure whether he would stay and finish or rush off to be with his wife. I had to think about messing with his personal life or making certain his work was done on time. The moral dilemma came down to one issue: What were a few more weeks of their separation when the whole world could benefit for years to come from his research?" From the corner of his eye he could see her nodding.

"I understand. I might have done the same thing under the circumstances. But why didn't you explain this to me?"

"Because of your gung-ho efforts to reunite Tony and his wife, I thought you would insist I take you to Tony. Then I worried about you asking around San Remo about a free-lance botantist." He looked at her sharply. "The kind of botanist a pharmaceutical company might hire to do field research. The kind of botanist that we think El Diablo Timber had murdered last year."

"Tony told me," she said with a pained expression that distorted her features.

Scratching his head, Reilly stared at his nightstand before he continued. "Later on, when we . . . got closer, I kept wanting to tell you. Everytime I managed to get up the courage, you'd look up at me with those big blue eyes of yours and tell me how honest and good I was. Don't you see? I knew as soon as I told you, you'd probably have a fit." He heard the desperation in his voice but didn't try to mask it. What point would there be? He *was* desperate. "Al, we were having such a good time. Something had started happening to us. Something at age thirty-four I'd given up on ever finding. Something so strong and pure." He looked at her blue shorts and white camp shirt, fully and achingly aware of how feminine and sexy she was in the utilitarian outfit. "I think we'd both given up hope in the finding-the-perfect-mate department. Then we stumbled on each other and fell hard." He lowered his forehead to his hands and sighed. "I did not want it to end," he said emphatically, "so I put off telling you how much I knew. I hoped that the closer we became, the more chance I'd have of you accepting what I'd done. Or hadn't done as it turned out."

"But you let me get on that plane. You didn't try to stop me or explain any of this to me. You should have said something. You let me go all the way to Connecticut and spend two weeks in misery without knowing the truth. I ached, I was so lonely for you."

He lifted his head, shooting her a look of disbelief. "What about me? What was I supposed to think? The last thing you said to me was that our moment together was all childish fantasy." He reached over to his nightstand and opened the drawer. "Like I said, it wasn't a fantasy to me," he said, reaching in and carefully taking out her braid. "I went back upriver and begged this off the chief. I've slept with your hair on my pillow for over a week now. It still carries your scent," he said, before closing his eyes and breathing in slowly. The poignancy of his own gesture left his voice raw with emotion. "Hell, I even had to wrestle Puddin' Head for it one night."

"Reilly," she whispered, her voice cracking with tense laughter. She walked over to him, mussing his hair. "Did you really?"

"Really." He pulled her into his lap, burying his cheek against her breasts. "I love you, Al," he said, marveling at the woman in his arms. "And I swear, from this moment on, I'll never hold back anything from you again."

She lifted his face, bringing it to hers in both hands. "I believe you," she said, pressing a sumptuous kiss to his mouth. His hands moved to her waist, massaging the inward curves as he deepened the kiss. Nothing had ever felt so right. After a while she lifted her mouth from his. "I thought you were sticking around here to make improvements on the hotel with Chico's father."

"I thought so, too, but Taylor Pharmaceuticals wants a new face in Paradise. Jack Stratford, to be exact."

Smoothing her thumbs along the corners of his mouth, she lifted her gaze to his eyes. His cautious look prompted her to ask, "Where do they want *you*?"

"Brazil."

"Brazil," she repeated with a faraway look in her eyes. She stood up slowly.

He held his breath. "Al?"

Repositioning herself, she straddled Reilly's lap and sat down again. "Isn't that where they do that sexy dance? You know the one," she said, providing him with a few choice moves.

His physical reaction was fast and to the

point as she moved to center herself over him. "Whatever happened to that lady in the white linen suit?" he asked, unbuttoning her blouse.

"You tell me," she said, tracing exotic patterns in Reilly's chest hair.

"She quit her job and ran away to live in the jungle with Tarzan," he said, peeling the blouse down her arms. Throwing it across the room, he added, "And no one ever heard from her again."

"No kidding," Allison whispered, dropping her head back to accept the kiss he pressed to the swelling curve of her right breast. And then to her left. "How did Tarzan manage that?"

"He promised her paradise for the rest of her life, if she'd change her name to Mrs. Anderson. Did I mention that Reverend Phillips is licensed to perform weddings?"

She shook her head.

"Al?" His voice was a tender whisper, totally devoid of the playful quality he'd just used. "This is no fantasy. I mean what I'm saying. Will you marry me?" He pressed two fingers to her lips. "Wait. Will you marry me tonight?"

She stood up again. "Yes. And yes. Oh, Lord, Reilly, we have a million things to do."

He stood up too. "You're not kidding. I'll

have to get in touch with the main office to let them know there will be two of us going. And you haven't met my family yet."

"And I promised Susan I'd let her know what happened as soon as I talked to you. And then I—" She stopped and made a face at him. "We're sounding extremely responsible, aren't we?"

They looked at each other, nodding together until the nod turned into a slow shake of their heads. "Later," he said as his hands went for the zipper on his pants.

"Much later," she agreed, slipping out of the rest of her clothes. "Reilly? You didn't ask what that lady in the white linen suit promised Tarzan in return."

"What was that?"

"Not to be afraid," she said, climbing onto the bed. He climbed in with her, and they pulled the mosquito netting into place. "To be in this moment," she said, running her fingers through his hair. "And to be spontaneous. To always be spontaneous." She laughed softly against his cheek.

"What are you laughing at?"

"I've never made love to a man with hair longer than mine."

"Well, I'm sure you'll do fine," he said, drawing her down beside him. "After all, Jane did it for Tarzan."

THE EDITOR'S CORNER

Let the fires of love's passion keep you warm as summer's days shorten into the frosty nights of autumn. Those falling leaves and chilly mornings are a sure signal that winter's on the way! So make a date to snuggle up under a comforter and read the six romances LOVESWEPT has in store for you. They're sure to heat up your reading hours with their witty and sensuous tales.

Fayrene Preston's scrumptious and clever story, **THE COLORS OF JOY**, LOVESWEPT #642 is a surefire heartwarmer. Seemingly unaware of his surroundings, Caleb McClintock steps off the curb—and is yanked out of the path of an oncoming car by a blue-eyed angel! Even though Joy Williams had been pretending to be her twin sister as part of a daredevil charade, he'd recognized her, known her when almost no one could tell them apart. His wickedly sensual experiments will surely show a lady who's adored variety that one man is all she'll ever need! You won't soon forget this charming story by Fayrene.

Take a trip to the tropics with Linda Wisdom's **SUDDEN IMPULSE**, LOVESWEPT #643. Ben Wyatt had imagined the creator of vivid fabric designs as a passionate wanton who wove her fiery fantasies into the cloth of dreams, but when he flew to Treasure Cove to meet her, he was shocked to encounter Kelly Andrews, a cool businesswoman who'd chosen paradise as an escape! Beguiled by the tawny-eyed designer who'd sworn off driven men wedded to their work, Ben sensed that beneath her silken surface was a fire he must taste. Captivated by her beauty, enthralled by her sensuality, Ben challenged her to seize her chance at love. Linda's steamy tale will melt away the frost of a chilly autumn day.

Theresa Gladden will get you in the Halloween mood with her spooky but oh, so sexy duo, **ANGIE AND THE GHOSTBUSTER**, LOVESWEPT #644. Drawn to an old house by an intriguing letter and a shockingly vivid dream, Dr. Gabriel Richards came in search of a tormented ghost—but instead found a sassy blonde with dreamer's eyes who awakened an old torment of his own. Angie Parker was two-parts angel to one-part vixen, a sexy, skeptical, single mom who suspected a con—but couldn't deny the chemistry between them, or disguise her burning need. Theresa puts her "supernatural" talents to their best use in this delightful tale.

The ever-creative and talented Judy Gill returns with a magnificent, touching tale that I'm sure you'll agree is a **SHEER DELIGHT**, LOVESWEPT #645. Matt Fiedler had been caught looking—and touching—the silky lingerie on display in the sweet-scented boutique, but when he discovered he'd stumbled into Dee Farris's shop, he wanted his hands all over the lady instead! Dee had never forgotten the reckless bad boy who'd awakened her to exquisite passion in college, then shattered her dreams by promising to return for her, but never keeping his word. Dee feared the doubts that had once driven him away couldn't be silenced by desire, that Matt's pride might be stronger than his need to possess her. This one will grab hold of your heartstrings and never let go!

Victoria Leigh's in brilliant form with **TAKE A CHANCE ON LOVE**, LOVESWEPT #646. Biff Fuller could almost taste her skin and smell her exotic fragrance from across the casino floor, but he sensed that the bare-shouldered woman gambling with such abandon might be the most dangerous risk he'd ever taken! Amanda Lawrence never expected to see him again, the man who'd branded her his with only a touch. But when Biff appeared without warning and vowed to fight her dragons, she had to surrender. The emotional tension in Vicki's very special story will leave you breathless!

I'm sure that you must have loved Bonnie Pega's first book with us last summer. I'm happy to say that she's outdoing herself with her second great love story, **WILD THING**, LOVESWEPT #647. Patrick Brady knew he'd had a concussion, but was the woman he saw only a hazy fantasy, or delectable flesh and blood? Robin McKenna wasn't thrilled about caring for the man, even less when she learned her handsome patient was a reporter—but she was helpless to resist his long, lean body and his wicked grin. Seduced by searing embraces and tantalized by unbearable longing, Robin wondered if she dared confess the truth. Trusting Patrick meant surrendering her sorrow, but could he show her she was brave enough to claim his love forever? Bonnie's on her way to becoming one of your LOVESWEPT favorites with **WILD THING**.

Here's to the fresh, cool days—and hot nights—of fall.

With best wishes,

Nita Taublib

Nita Taublib
Associate Publisher

P.S. Don't miss the exciting big women's fiction reads Bantam will have on sale in September: Teresa Medeiros's **A WHISPER OF ROSES,** Rosanne Bittner's **TENDER BETRAYAL,** Lucia Grahame's **THE PAINTED LADY,** and Sara Orwig's **OREGON BROWN.** We'll be giving you a sneak peek at these terrific books in next month's LOVESWEPTS. And immediately following this page look for a preview of the spectacular women's fiction books from Bantam *available now!*

Don't miss these exciting books by your
favorite Bantam authors

On sale in August:
*THE MAGNIFICENT
ROGUE*
by Iris Johansen

VIRTUE
by Jane Feather

*BENEATH A SAPPHIRE
SEA*
by Jessica Bryan

TEMPTING EDEN
by Maureen Reynolds

And in hardcover from Doubleday
WHERE DOLPHINS GO
by Peggy Webb

Iris Johansen

nationally bestselling author of
THE TIGER PRINCE

presents

THE MAGNIFICENT ROGUE

Iris Johansen's spellbinding, sensuous romantic novels have captivated readers and won awards for a decade now, and this is her most spectacular story yet. From the glittering court of Queen Elizabeth to a barren Scottish island, here is a heartstopping tale of courageous love . . . and unspeakable evil.

The daring chieftain of a Scottish clan, Robert McDarren knows no fear, and only the threat to a kinsman's life makes him bow to Queen Elizabeth's order that he wed Kathryn Ann Kentrye. He's aware of the dangerous secret in Kate's past, a secret that could destroy a great empire, but he doesn't expect the stirring of desire when he first lays eyes on the fragile beauty. Grateful to escape the tyranny of her guardian, Kate accepts the mesmerizing stranger as her husband. But even as they discover a passion greater than either has known, enemies are weaving their poisonous web around them, and soon Robert and Kate must risk their very lives to defy the ultimate treachery.

"I won't hush. You cannot push me away again. I tell you that—"

Robert covered her lips with his hand. "I know what you're saying. You're saying I don't have to shelter you under my wing but I must coo like a peaceful dove whenever I'm around you."

"I could not imagine you cooing, but I do not think peace and friendship between us is too much to ask." She blinked rapidly as she moved her head to avoid his hand. "You promised that—"

"I know what I promised and you have no right to ask more from me. You can't expect to beckon me close and then have me keep my distance," he said harshly. "You can't have it both ways, as you would know if you weren't—" He broke off. "And for God's sake don't *weep*."

"I'm not weeping."

"By God, you are."

"I have something in my eye. You're not being sensible."

"I'm being more sensible than you know," he said with exasperation. "Christ, why the devil is this so important to you?"

She wasn't sure except that it had something to do with that wondrous feeling of *rightness* she had experienced last night. She had never known it before and she would not give it up. She tried to put it into words. "I feel as if I've been closed up inside for a long time. Now I want . . . something else. It will do you no harm to be my friend."

"That's not all you want," he said slowly as he studied her desperate expression. "I don't think you know what you want. But I do and I can't give it to you."

"You could try." She drew a deep breath. "Do you think it's easy for me to ask this of you? It fills me with anger and helplessness and I *hate* that feeling."

She wasn't reaching him. She had to say something that would convince him. Suddenly the words came tumbling out, words she had never meant to say, expressing emotions she had never realized she felt. "I thought all I'd need would be a house but now I know there's something more. I have to have people too. I guess I always knew it but the house was easier, safer. Can't you see? I want what you and Gavin and Angus have, and I don't know if I can find it alone. Sebastian told me I couldn't have it but I will. I *will*." Her hands nervously clenched and unclenched at her sides. "I'm all tight inside. I feel scorched . . . like a desert. Sebastian made me this way and I don't know how to stop. I'm not . . . at ease with anyone."

He smiled ironically. "I've noticed a certain lack of trust in me but you seem to have no problem with Gavin."

"I truly like Gavin but he can't change what I am," she answered, then went on eagerly. "It was different with you last night, though. I really *talked* to you. You made me feel . . ." She stopped. She had sacrificed enough of her pride. If this was not enough, she could give no more.

The only emotion she could identify in the multitude of expressions that flickered across his face was frustration. And there was something else, something darker, more intense. He threw up his hands. "All right, I'll try."

Joy flooded through her. "Truly?"

"My God, you're obstinate."

"It's the only way to keep what one has. If I hadn't fought, you'd have walked away."

"I see." She had the uneasy feeling he saw more than her words had portended. But she must accept this subtle intrusion of apprehension if she was to be fully accepted by him.

"Do I have to make a solemn vow?" he asked with a quizzical lift of his brows.

"Yes, please. Truly?" she persisted.

"Truly." Some of the exasperation left his face. "Satisfied?"

"Yes, that's all I want."

"Is it?" He smiled crookedly. "That's not all I want."

The air between them was suddenly thick and hard to breathe, and Kate could feel the heat burn in her cheeks. She swallowed. "I'm sure you'll get over that once you become accustomed to thinking of me differently."

He didn't answer.

"You'll see." She smiled determinedly and quickly changed the subject. "Where is Gavin?"

"In the kitchen fetching food for the trail."

"I'll go find him and tell him you wish to leave at—"

"In a moment." He moved to stand in front of her and lifted the hood of her cape, then framed her face with a gesture that held a possessive intimacy. He looked down at her, holding her gaze. "This is not a wise thing. I don't know how long I can stand this box you've put me in. All I can promise is that I'll give you warning when I decide to break down the walls."

VIRTUE
by
Jane Feather

"GOLD 5 stars." —*Heartland Critiques*

"An instantaneous attention-grabber. A well-crafted romance with a strong, compelling story and utterly delightful characters." —*Romantic Times*

VIRTUE is the newest regency romance from Jane Feather, four-time winner of Romantic Times's *Reviewer's Choice award, and author of the national bestseller* The Eagle and the Dove.

With a highly sensual style reminiscent of Amanda Quick and Karen Robards, Jane Feather works her bestselling romantic magic with this tale of a strong-willed beauty forced to make her living at the gaming tables, and the arrogant nobleman determined to get the better of her—with passion. The stakes are nothing less than her VIRTUE . . .

What the devil was she doing? Marcus Devlin, the most honorable Marquis of Carrington, absently exchanged his empty champagne glass for a full one as a flunkey passed him. He pushed his shoulders off the wall, straightening to his full height, the better to see across the crowded room to the macao table. She was up to something. Every prickling hair on the nape of his neck told him so.

She was standing behind Charlie's chair, her fan moving in slow sweeps across the lower part of her face. She leaned forward to whisper something in Charlie's ear, and the rich swell of her breasts, the deep shadow of the cleft between them, was uninhibitedly revealed in the décolletage of her evening gown. Charlie looked up at her and smiled, the soft, infatuated smile of puppy love. It wasn't surprising this young cousin had fallen head over heels for Miss Judith Davenport, the marquis reflected. There was hardly a man in Brussels who wasn't stirred by her: a creature of opposites, vibrant, ebullient, sharply intelligent—a woman who in some indefinable fashion challenged a man, put him on his mettle one minute, and yet the next was as appealing as a kitten; a man wanted to pick her up and cuddle her, protect her from the storm . . .

Romantic nonsense! The marquis castigated himself severely for sounding like his cousin and half the young soldiers proudly sporting their regimentals in the salons of Brussels as the world waited for Napoleon to make his move. He'd been watching Judith Davenport weaving her spells for several weeks now, convinced she was an artful minx with a very clear agenda of her own. But for the life of him, he couldn't discover what it was.

His eyes rested on the young man sitting opposite Charlie. Sebastian Davenport held the bank. As beautiful as his sister in his own way, he sprawled in his chair, both clothing and posture radiating a studied carelessness. He was laughing across the table, lightly ruffling the cards in his hands. The mood at the table was lighthearted. It was a mood that always accompanied the Davenports. Presumably one reason why they were so popular . . . and then the marquis saw it.

It was the movement of her fan. There was a pattern to the slow sweeping motion. Sometimes the movement speeded, sometimes it paused, once or twice she snapped the fan closed, then almost immediately began a more vigorous wafting of the delicately painted half moon. There was renewed laughter at the table, and with a lazy sweep of his rake, Sebastian Davenport scooped toward him the pile of vowels and rouleaux in the center of the table.

The marquis walked across the room. As he reached the table, Charlie looked up with a rueful grin. "It's not my night, Marcus."

"It rarely is," Carrington said, taking snuff. "Be careful you don't find yourself in debt." Charlie heard the warning in the advice, for all that his cousin's voice was affably casual. A slight flush tinged the young man's cheekbones and he dropped his eyes to his cards again. Marcus was his guardian and tended to be unsympathetic when Charlie's gaming debts outran his quarterly allowance.

"Do you care to play, Lord Carrington?" Judith Davenport's soft voice spoke at the marquis's shoulder and he turned to look at her. She was smiling, her golden brown eyes luminous, framed in the thickest, curliest eyelashes he had ever seen. However, ten years spent avoiding the frequently blatant blandishments of maidens on the lookout for a rich husband had inured him to the cajolery of a pair of fine eyes.

"No. I suspect it wouldn't be my night either, Miss Davenport. *May* I escort you to the supper room? It must grow tedious, watching my cousin losing hand over fist." He offered a small bow and took her elbow without waiting for a response.

Judith stiffened, feeling the pressure of his hand cupping her bare arm. There was a hardness in his eyes that matched the firmness of his grip, and her scalp contracted as unease shivered across her skin. "On the contrary, my lord, I find the play most entertaining." She gave her arm a covert, experimental tug. His fingers gripped warmly and yet more firmly.

"But I insist, Miss Davenport. You will enjoy a glass of negus."

He had very black eyes and they carried a most unpleasant glitter, as insistent as his tone and words, both of which were drawing a degree of puzzled attention. Judith could see no discreet, graceful escape route. She laughed lightly. "You have convinced me, sir. But I prefer burnt champagne to negus."

"Easily arranged." He drew her arm through his and laid his free hand over hers, resting on his black silk sleeve. Judith felt manacled.

They walked through the card room in a silence that was as uncomfortable as it was pregnant. Had he guessed what was going on? Had he seen anything? How could she have given herself away? Or was it something Sebastian had done, said, looked . . . ? The questions and speculations raced through Judith's brain. She was barely acquainted with Marcus Devlin. He was too sophisticated, too hardheaded to be of use to herself and Sebastian, but she had the distinct sense that he would be an opponent to be reckoned with.

The supper room lay beyond the ballroom, but instead of guiding his companion around the waltzing couples and the ranks of seated chaperones against the wall, Marcus turned aside toward the long French windows opening onto a flagged terrace. A breeze stirred the heavy velvet curtains over an open door.

"I was under the impression we were going to have supper." Judith stopped abruptly.

"No, we're going to take a stroll in the night air," her escort informed her with a bland smile. "Do put one foot in front of the other, my dear ma'am, otherwise our progress might become a little uneven." An unmistakable jerk on her arm drew her forward with a stumble, and Judith rapidly adjusted her gait to match the leisured, purposeful stroll of her companion.

"I don't care for the night air," she hissed through her teeth, keeping a smile on her face. "It's very bad for the constitution and frequently results in the ague or rheumatism."

"Only for those in their dotage," he said, lifting thick black eyebrows. "I would have said you were not a day above twenty-two. Unless you're very skilled with powder and paint?"

He'd pinpointed her age exactly and the sense of being dismayingly out of her depth was intensified. "I'm not quite such an accomplished actress, my lord," she said coldly.

"Are you not?" He held the curtain aside for her and she found herself out on the terrace, lit by flambeaux set in sconces at intervals along the low parapet fronting the sweep of green lawn. "I would have sworn you were as accomplished as any on Drury Lane." The statement was accompanied by a penetrating stare.

Judith rallied her forces and responded to the comment as if it were a humorous compliment. "You're too kind, sir. I confess I've long envied the talent of Mrs. Siddons."

"Oh, you underestimate yourself," he said softly. They had reached the parapet and he stopped under the light of a torch. "You are playing some very pretty theatricals, Miss Davenport, you and your brother."

Judith drew herself up to her full height. It wasn't a

particularly impressive move when compared with her escort's breadth and stature, but it gave her an illusion of hauteur. "I don't know what you're talking about, my lord. It seems you've obliged me to accompany you in order to insult me with vague innuendoes."

"No, there's nothing vague about my accusations," he said. "However insulting they may be. I am assuming my cousin's card play will improve in your absence."

"What are you implying?" The color ebbed in her cheeks, then flooded back in a hot and revealing wave. Hastily she employed her fan in an effort to conceal her agitation.

The marquis caught her wrist and deftly twisted the fan from her hand. "You're most expert with a fan, madam."

"I beg your pardon?" She tried again for a lofty incomprehension, but with increasing lack of conviction.

"Don't continue this charade, Miss Davenport. It benefits neither of us. You and your brother may fleece as many fools as you can find as far as I'm concerned, but you'll leave my cousin alone."

Beneath a Sapphire Sea
by
Jessica Bryan
Rave reviews for Ms. Bryan's novels:

*Beneath the shimmering, sunlit surface of the ocean there
lives a race of rare and wondrous men and women. They
have walked upon the land, but their true heritage is as
beings of the sea. Now their people face a grave peril. And
one woman holds the key to their survival. . . .*

*A scholar of sea lore, Meredith came to a Greek island to
follow her academic pursuits. But when she encountered
Galen, a proud, determined warrior of the sea, she was
eternally linked with a world far more elusive and mysteri-
ously seductive than her own. For she alone possessed a scroll
that held the secrets of his people.*

*In the following scene, Meredith has just caught Galen
searching for the mysterious scroll. His reaction catches them
both by surprise . . .*

He drew her closer, and Meredith did not resist. To look
away from his face had become impossible. She felt something in him reach out for her, and something in her

answered. It rose up in her like a tide, compelling beyond reason or thought. She lifted her arms and slowly put them around his broad shoulders. He tensed, as if she had startled him, then his whole body seemed to envelop hers as he pulled her against him and lowered his lips to hers.

His arms were like bands of steel, the thud of his heart deep and powerful as a drum, beating in a wild rhythm that echoed the same frantic cadence of Meredith's. His lips seared over hers. His breath was hot in her mouth, and the hard muscles of his bare upper thighs thrust against her lower belly, the bulge between them only lightly concealed by the thin material of his shorts.

Then, as quickly as their lips had come together, they parted.

Galen stared down into Meredith's face, his arms still locked around her slim, strong back. He was deeply shaken, far more than he cared to admit, even to himself. He had been totally focused on probing the landwoman's mind once and for all. Where had the driving urge to kiss her come from, descending on him with a need so strong it had overridden everything else?

He dropped his arms. "That was a mistake," he said, frowning. "I—"

"You're right." Whatever had taken hold of Meredith vanished like the "pop" of a soap bubble, leaving her feeling as though she had fallen headfirst into a cold sea. "It *was* a mistake," she said quickly. "Mine. Now if you'll just get out of here, we can both forget this unfortunate incident ever happened."

She stepped back from him, and Galen saw the anger in her eyes and, held deep below that anger, the hurt. It stung him. None of this was her fault. Whatever forces she exerted upon him, he was convinced she was completely unaware of them. He was equally certain she had no idea of the scroll's significance. To her it was simply an impressive artifact, a rare find that would no doubt gain her great recognition in this folklore profession of hers.

He could not allow that, of course. But the methods he had expected to succeed with her had not worked. He could try again—the very thought of pulling her back into her arms was a seductive one. It played on his senses with heady anticipation, shocking him at how easily this woman could distract him. He would have to find another less physical means of discovering where the scroll was.

"I did not mean it that way," he began in a gentle tone.

Meredith shook her head, refusing to be mollified. She was as taken aback as he by what had happened, and deeply chagrined as well. The fact that she had enjoyed the kiss—No, that was too calm a way of describing it. Galen's mouth had sent rivers of sensations coursing through her, sensations she had not known existed, and that just made the chagrin worse.

"I don't care what you meant," she said in a voice as stiff as her posture. "I've asked you to leave. I don't want to tell you again."

"Meredith, wait." He stepped forward, stopping just short of touching her. "I'm sorry about . . . Please believe my last wish is to offend you. But it does not change the fact that I still want to work with you. And whether you admit it or not, you need me."

"Need you?" Her tone grew frosty. "I don't see how."

"Then you don't see very much," he snapped. He paused to draw in a deep breath, then continued in a placating tone. "Who else can interpret the language on this sheet of paper for you?"

Meredith eyed him. If he was telling the truth, if he really could make sense out on those characters, then, despite the problems he presented, he was an answer to her prayers, to this obsession that would not let her go. She bent and picked up the fallen piece of paper.

"Prove it." She held it out to him. "What does this say?"

He ignored the paper, staring steadily at her. "We will work together, then?"

She frowned as she returned his stare, trying to probe whatever lay behind his handsome face. "Why is it so important to you that we do? I can see why you might think I need you, but what do you get out of this? What do you want, Galen?"

He took the paper from her. "*The season of destruction will soon be upon us and our city,*" he read deliberately, "*but I may have found a way to save some of us, we who were once among the most powerful in the sea. Near the long and narrow island that is but a stone's throw from Crete, the island split by Mother Ocean into two halves . . .*"

He stopped. "It ends there." His voice was low and fierce, as fierce as his gaze, which seemed to reach out to grip her. "Are you satisfied now? Or do you require still more proof?"

TEMPTING EDEN
by
Maureen Reynolds

author of SMOKE EYES

"Ms. Reynolds blends steamy sensuality with
marvelous lovers. . . . delightful."
—*Romantic Times on SMOKE EYES*

*Eden Victoria Lindsay knew it was foolish to break into the
home of one of New York's most famous—and reclusive—
private investigators. Now she had fifteen minutes to convince him that he shouldn't have her thrown in prison.*

*Shane O'Connor hardly knew what to make of the flaxen-
haired aristocrat who'd scaled the wall of his Long Island
mansion—except that she was in more danger than she
suspected. In his line of work, trusting the wrong woman
could get a man killed, but Shane is about to himself get
taken in by this alluring and unconventional beauty. . . .*

"She scaled the wall, sir," said Simon, Shane's stern
butler.

Eden rolled her eyes. "Yes—yes, I did! And I'd do it
again—a hundred times. How else could I reach the
impossible *inaccessible* Mr. O'Connor?"

He watched her with a quiet intensity but it was Simon
who answered, "If one wishes to speak with Mr. O'Connor, a meeting is usually arranged through the *proper*
channels."

Honestly, Eden thought, the English aristocracy did
not look down their noses half so well as these two!

O'Connor stepped gracefully out of the light and his

gaze, falling upon her, was like the steel of gunmetal. He leaned casually against the wall—his weight on one hip, his hands in his trousers pockets—and he studied her with half-veiled eyes.

"Have you informed the . . . ah . . . *lady*, Simon, what type of reception our unexpected guests might anticipate? Especially," he added in a deceptively soft tone, "those who scale the estate walls, and . . . er . . . shed their clothing?"

Eden stiffened, her face hot with color; he'd made it sound as if it were *commonplace* for women to scale his wall and undress.

Simon replied, "Ah, no, sir. In the melee, that particular formality slipped my mind."

"Do you suppose we should strip her first, or just torture her?"

"*What?*"

"Or would you rather we just arrest you, madame?"

"Sir, with your attitude it is a wonder you have a practice at all!"

"It is a wonder," he drawled coldly, "that you are still alive, madame. You're a damn fool to risk your neck as you did. Men have been shot merely for attempting it, and I'm amazed you weren't killed yourself."

Eden brightened. "Then I am to be commended, am I not? Congratulate me, sir, for accomplishing such a feat!"

Shane stared at her as if she were daft.

"And for my prowess you should be more than willing to give me your time. Please, just listen to my story! I promise I will pay you handsomely for your time!"

As her eyes met his, Eden began to feel hope seep from her. At her impassioned plea there was no softening in his chiseled features, or in his stony gaze. In a final attempt she gave him her most imploring look, and then instantly regretted it, for the light in his eyes suddenly burned brighter. It was as if he knew her game.

"State your business," O'Connor bit out.

"I need you to find my twin brother."

Shane frowned. "You have a twin?"

"Yes I do."

God help the world, he thought.

He leaned to crush out his cheroot, his gaze watching

her with a burning, probing intensity. "*Why* do you need me to find your twin?"

"Because he's missing, of course," she said in a mildly exasperated voice.

Shane brought his thumb and forefinger up to knead the bridge of his nose. "*Why*, do you need me to find him? *Why* do you think he is missing, and not on some drunken spree entertaining the . . . uh . . . 'ladies'?"

"Well, Mr. O'Connor, that's very astute of you— excuse me, do you have a headache, sir?"

"Not yet."

Eden hurried on. "Actually I might agree with you that Philip could be on a drunken spree, but the circumstances surrounding his disappearance don't match that observation."

Shane lifted a brow.

"You see, Philip *does* spend a good deal of time in the brothels, and there are three in particular that he frequents. But the madames of all of them told me they haven't seen him for several days."

Shane gave her a strange look. "You went into a brothel?"

"No. I went into *three*. And Philip wasn't in any of them." She thought she caught the tiniest flicker of amusement in his silver eyes, then quickly dismissed the notion. Unlikely the man had a drop of mirth in him.

"What do you mean by 'the circumstances matching the observation'?"

Eden suddenly realized she had not produced a shred of evidence. "Please turn around and look away from me Mr. O'Connor."

"Like hell."

Though her heart thudded hard, Eden smiled radiantly. "But you must! You have to!"

"I don't *have* to do anything I don't damn well please, madame."

"Please, Mr. O'Connor." Her tearing eyes betrayed her guise of confidence. "I-I brought some evidence I think might help you with the case—that is if you take it. But it's—I had to carry it under my skirt. Please," she begged softly.

Faintly amused, Shane shifted his gaze out toward the bay. Out of the corner of his eye he saw her twirl around, hoist her layers of petticoats to her waist, and fumble with something.

She turned around again, and with a dramatic flair that was completely artless, she opened the chamois bag she had tied to the waistband of her pantalets. She grabbed his hand and plopped a huge, uncut diamond into the center of his palm. Then she took hold of his other hand and plunked down another stone—an extraordinary grass-green emerald as large as the enormous diamond.

"Where," he asked in a hard drawl, "did you get these?"

"That," Eden said, "is what I've come to tell you."

OFFICIAL RULES

To enter the sweepstakes below carefully follow all instructions found elsewhere in this offer.

The **Winners Classic** will award prizes with the following approximate maximum values: 1 Grand Prize: $26,500 (or $25,000 cash alternate); 1 First Prize: $3,000; 5 Second Prizes: $400 each; 35 Third Prizes: $100 each; 1,000 Fourth Prizes: $7.50 each. Total maximum retail value of Winners Classic Sweepstakes is $42,500. Some presentations of this sweepstakes may contain individual entry numbers corresponding to one or more of the aforementioned prize levels. To determine the Winners, individual entry numbers will first be compared with the winning numbers preselected by computer. For winning numbers not returned, prizes will be awarded in random drawings from among all eligible entries received. Prize choices may be offered at various levels. If a winner chooses an automobile prize, all license and registration fees, taxes, destination charges and, other expenses not offered herein are the responsibility of the winner. If a winner chooses a trip, travel must be complete within one year from the time the prize is awarded. Minors must be accompanied by an adult. Travel companion(s) must also sign release of liability. Trips are subject to space and departure availability. Certain black-out dates may apply.

The following applies to the sweepstakes named above:

No purchase necessary. You can also enter the sweepstakes by sending your name and address to: P.O. Box 508, Gibbstown, N.J. 08027. Mail each entry separately. Sweepstakes begins 6/1/93. Entries must be received by 12/30/94. Not responsible for lost, late, damaged, misdirected, illegible or postage due mail. Mechanically reproduced entries are not eligible. All entries become property of the sponsor and will not be returned.

Prize Selection/Validations: Selection of winners will be conducted no later than 5:00 PM on January 28, 1995, by an independent judging organization whose decisions are final. Random drawings will be held at 1211 Avenue of the Americas, New York, N.Y. 10036. Entrants need not be present to win. Odds of winning are determined by total number of entries received. Circulation of this sweepstakes is estimated not to exceed 200 million. All prizes are guaranteed to be awarded and delivered to winners. Winners will be notified by mail and may be required to complete an affidavit of eligibility and release of liability which must be returned within 14 days of date on notification or alternate winners will be selected in a random drawing. Any prize notification letter or any prize returned to a participating sponsor, Bantam Doubleday Dell Publishing Group, Inc., its participating divisions or subsidiaries, or the independent judging organization as undeliverable will be awarded to an alternate winner. Prizes are not transferable. No substitution for prizes except as offered or as may be necessary due to unavailability, in which case a prize of equal or greater value will be awarded. Prizes will be awarded approximately 90 days after the drawing. All taxes are the sole responsibility of the winners. Entry constitutes permission (except where prohibited by law) to use winners' names, hometowns, and likenesses for publicity purposes without further or other compensation. Prizes won by minors will be awarded in the name of parent or legal guardian.

Participation: Sweepstakes open to residents of the United States and Canada, except for the province of Quebec. Sweepstakes sponsored by Bantam Doubleday Dell Publishing Group, Inc., (BDD), 1540 Broadway, New York, NY 10036. Versions of this sweepstakes with different graphics and prize choices will be offered in conjunction with various solicitations or promotions by different subsidiaries and divisions of BDD. Where applicable, winners will have their choice of any prize offered at level won. Employees of BDD, its divisions, subsidiaries, advertising agencies, independent judging organization, and their immediate family members are not eligible.

Canadian residents, in order to win, must first correctly answer a time limited arithmetical skill testing question. Void in Puerto Rico, Quebec and wherever prohibited or restricted by law. Subject to all federal, state, local and provincial laws and regulations. For a list of major prize winners (available after 1/29/95): send a self-addressed, stamped envelope entirely separate from your entry to: Sweepstakes Winners, P.O. Box 517, Gibbstown, NJ 08027. Requests must be received by 12/30/94. DO NOT SEND ANY OTHER CORRESPONDENCE TO THIS P.O. BOX.

Don't miss these fabulous Bantam women's fiction titles on sale in September